HONOR BOUND

Guardians of the Fae Realms: Book 11
JL Madore

CHAPTER ONE

Honor

"I am Honor Thornebane, Princess of Dornte, Guardian of the Crown. Thank you all for coming to help us during this time of turmoil. Who's in charge?"

The attention of the men gathered in the castle cafeteria shifts toward a well-built and chiseled man with a mop of shoulder-length, russet red curls. "That would be me, lass. Connor MacDougall at yer service, but most people call me Mac. How can we help?"

"How much do you know about why you're here?"

"Och, bits and bobs, mostly. It seems there's an uprisin' underway and yer military forces have been left wanton."

"Unfortunately, yes. Without going into a history lesson, the members of my family are the rightful rulers of this quadrant. There is a group of wealthy citizens who want to shift the ruling power from the people to the one-percenters. We can't let that happen."

"And what do ye need from us to squash it?"

"As you mentioned, our military forces have been depleted.

A skirmish in the chapel a moment ago alerted us to hostiles within the castle. I want a team with me searching for the traitors. At the same time, I need to send reinforcements to all the entrances and exits to ensure we don't have any other surprise guests."

"Ye had men on the doors when we arrived. Has somethin' happened to them?"

"No, but your men won't have any interest in switching sides during the commotion. I can't say the same for all of our citizens."

"How many exits do we need to cover?"

"In total, there are eight possible ways to enter the castle without smashing a hole through a wall. Protective screens were lowered on the windows, and portaling is being heavily warded against, so the doors should be our only point of entry. Our first objective is to secure the castle. Once that's complete, we'll send teams out to the grounds to secure the raiding rebels."

"What about those wee monsters shootin' knock-out darts? I like a game of sport as much as the next fella, but would rather not have my men in the crossfire of tarantulas having a tantrum."

"Understood. These dermal tags carry a frequency the sentinels recognize as a friend and not a foe. Pass them out to your men and stick them on your skin. After that, you should be good to go."

"Should be?" Connor Mac repeats.

I shrug. "This is our first chance to use them. Let's hope your Mr. Barron is as good as everyone says."

"Och, weel, if Mr. Barron is behind those wee bastards, I have all the confidence in the world." He takes the package and laughs. "Avengers?"

I roll my eyes at the printed superhero designs on the military tags. "Mr. Barron's mate, Brant, oversaw the design.

According to what I've been told, he thought these were better than standard issue."

Connor Mac laughs. "Och, I know the bear well. Enough said."

While Connor passes those off and the patches are distributed and stuck in place, I address my next problem. "Does anyone have contact with the incoming shuttle with the last group of officers through the Portal Gate? If they arrive and engage out on the lawns, they'll end up as paralyzed as the attackers."

Connor Mac extends his hand and snaps his fingers. "Brady, bring me yer radio, will ye?"

One of the soldiers at the nearby table breaks away from his group to deliver a hand-held radio to his commander.

"What frequency are we using for transportation?"

Someone sitting at the next table yells the answer and Connor Mac makes the necessary adjustments. "This is Alpha-1 calling Beta team. What's your ETA?"

"Beta-5 responding, sir. Two minutes out."

"Officer, hand your radio over to yer commander. We have a situation."

The line goes quiet for a moment and then a woman is the next to speak. "This is Beta-1. What's the situation, Mac?"

"We've got rebel raiders attackin' and the castle lockdown procedures released mechanical drones on the grounds as a front line defense. If ye try to approach on foot, yer team will be knocked out by tranq darts."

"Good to know. What do you suggest?"

"How many on your team can fly or portal?"

"Three can fly. One can portal."

"All right. Have those who can get to the roof of the castle without using the grounds secure our perimeter from that vantage point. The rest of your team should hang back and secure the entrance until we call off the sentinels."

"Roger that, Alpha-1. Keep us informed."

With that settled, Connor divides the men into three groups: those who will reinforce the castle security and guard the entrances, those who will accompany me to track down any rebels within the castle, and those who will monitor the comings and goings in the public spaces to ensure the safety of our citizens within the castle.

"There are four designated shelter areas for castle staff and civilians during a lockdown." I step over to where a map of the castle floorplan has been pinned on a board for the soldiers' orientation.

With an extended arm, I point to where they need to focus. "They are the chapel, the courtyard, the recreation room, and the throne room. Everyone should be there by now, so if you encounter stragglers in the corridors, question who they are and escort them to one of those four locations."

"And if we meet with resistance?" one of the men calls out.

"Identify yourself as Thornebane reinforcements. If they resist your direction, consider them hostile and detain them here in the cafeteria until we have time to deal with them."

Connor looks around to ensure everyone is clear on my orders and then we get moving.

The best part of having Hawk's FCO forces here is we are far more prepared to resist an attack than Ruic Breard and his bastard followers thought we were.

Hopefully, that gives us the edge we need to put an end to their uprisings once and for all.

~

Tundra

With Lukas in my arms, I push off the ground, spread my wings, and launch toward the flames engulfing the roof of the burning barn. It's impossible to see a way out through the fire, but there is no other option.

My eyes sting with the burn of smoke but I can't close them and risk not finding our path. Part of the roof has collapsed—I know because it fell on me while I was trying to find Lukas.

Logic dictates, if it fell there is a hole above and I can find it.

The searing heat of the fire is incredible. My skin feels like it's bubbling and the singeing in my lungs is even worse.

The higher I go, the hotter it becomes. The air is black with smoke and yet the most vibrant orange I could imagine at the same time.

Crack. The sound of wood breaking free from the frame pushes me back to avoid the falling debris. The world is raining fire, but there's no time left.

With all the force I can muster, I pump my wings and push through the blanket of fire above. Tucking Lukas tight to my chest, I curl around him as I rise.

It's not graceful, but in the end, it doesn't need to be. My wing bangs against a flaming beam and knocks me spinning but I manage to keep my upward thrust and have my arms locked around Lukas.

When I'm free of the structure, I follow the shaft of smoke high into the night sky before breaking off.

It offends everything within me to leave the scene not knowing what happened to the other members of the team. Were they killed by the bomb? Captured by the enemy? Do they need a rescue as well?

An energy bolt from a blaster strikes me in the back as a second narrowly misses my head. I curse, rising higher. I can't fight with Lukas in my arms and he's in no condition for me to set him down to engage in battle.

No. My first responsibility is to secure Lukas and ensure my mate survives.

With that in mind, I level out and head toward the landing

spot where we left the helicopter. It makes sense that any enforcers who escaped the ambush would return there to regroup.

Unsure what I will find back at the helicopter, I stay high in the clouds and don't give away my position.

It makes sense that if the opponents who attacked us knew we were coming, they likely were watching and awaiting our arrival.

They'd know where we landed our vehicle.

From my vantage point, high in the clouds, I don't see anything to suggest anyone is lying in wait but my instincts say differently. There's no sense risking Lukas's life down there.

He can't pilot the mechanical bird anyway.

Deciding to err on the side of caution, I bank south and search for a private area to take shelter. Lukas is much too still in my arms and the smell of char mixed with blood is sickening.

But where can I tend to him?

I scan the barren landscape searching for a place to land. There's nothing for a long while, but then the ground begins to rise and fall with outcroppings and sparse vegetation.

At first, it's only boulders and ground scrub but approximately three miles out, I spot a cluster of caves and descend to take a closer look.

Yes. This will work nicely.

Dune

It's interesting to be the fly on the wall or, in this case, the eyes in the sky. After locking myself into the oculus room at the top of Amberloq Hall, I've spent the past hour studying the intruders downstairs.

It didn't take long to realize the armed forces downstairs

aren't Thornebane military defenders. I may not know much about the Human Realm, but I realize that for them to pass as human in the general public, they have to at least look human or have glamor abilities.

As commonplace as green skin, neck gills, and faery wings are in this realm, seeing them on the fighting force downstairs makes it clear these soldiers are locals.

Staring into the reflection of the monitors, I look at myself and run things down. "Right. We're under attack, Amberloq Hall is the meeting place for the enemy, and I'm in the belly of the beast. Man, I'm glad I rushed back for this."

Actually, I *am* glad I rushed back for this.

Despite my protests, being a soldier for the Crown is all I ever wanted. Maybe I am the last Elbirfae from the Desert Plains Biome, but I'm still an Amberloq warrior.

It's my duty to protect the Thornebane rule.

Trying to contact the castle has been futile. If I'm right, the incoming raiders blocked all electronic signals with a jammer. There's no way for me to contact them or them to contact me using the castle system until that device is taken out.

Straightening, I ease back from the console and stretch out my wings. With the tips of my feathers brushing against the wall, I pace a slow circuit around the diameter of the cylindrical room.

I could fly back to the castle, but to do what? With the lockdown in place, there's not much I can do to help.

Staying here gives me the tactical advantage of infiltrating their ranks without them knowing.

Ha, look at me thinking things through.

It's easy to understand how these men ended up here. Those security drones were damn efficient at taking down the bulk of their forces. Finding shelter was the smartest course of action if they didn't want to end up playing the part of Thornebane lawn ornaments.

The questions now are… if these men are here, and another hundred or so are lying on the castle grass, what's happening inside the castle?

Did the lockdown prevent infiltration? Are Honor, Tundra, and Lukas battling together to keep the Thornebane Quad safe? Do they wish I was there to help?

Have they noticed that I'm not?

I roll my eyes and sigh. "Honor's right. I need to stop making everything about me. My insecurities get the better of me often and because of it, I act like an ass.

I need to do better.

I *will* do better.

If there's even a slight chance I can build a lasting relationship with Honor, I'll hit the self-improvement reset button and commit to overhauling my personality.

"That starts now." Turning my wrist over, I start pushing some of the buttons on my tactical watch. Tundra sent me the manual with the specs so I could learn how to use it, but I blew it off and figured my brilliance would shine through.

I'm barely able to tell the time on the stupid thing.

Pulling my tablet out from the thigh pocket of my tactical pants, I wake up the device and sign in. I may not be able to contact the castle with this, but I can read my files and learn how to use my watch.

I don't know a lot about the power signals that run these bad boys, but I bet my balls it's a different frequency than anything we have in this realm. And if I'm right, once I know how, I should be able to contact Honor inside the castle.

Oh, if Tundra could see me now…

"You win, Frosty. Here I am, studying hard. Better late than never, right?"

~

Shadow

I've always believed the best way for someone to forget about their problems is to help someone else fix theirs. It's one of the primary reasons I became a counselor in the first place. I enjoy helping others and I know what it's like to live with fears of what might be.

It's not always an easy job, and sometimes it's heartbreaking. Because no matter how good your intentions or how skilled you are at what you do, sometimes the situation is beyond your control.

"How is she doing?" I ask Keyla as the quadrant queen comes out of the guest suite.

She, Doc, and Jaxx have been in there for over an hour tending to Calli and her unborn young. I realize delivering a baby takes many hours, but when things first started to progress, there was a great deal of concern for not only the baby but for Calli as well.

"She's resting." Keyla sweeps her fingers across her forehead to gather the loose strands of chestnut hair that have escaped her ponytail. "The labor hasn't started yet, which Doc says is good. The longer she can hold off, the better our chance to figure out what's going wrong."

"What *is* going wrong?" I shift my wolf cub on my lap, rubbing under her chin to lift her gaze so I can read Keyla's expression. My bond with Moonshade, my little spirit wolf cub, is incredibly new but we are learning what each other needs faster than I expected.

Keyla sinks into the couch opposite me and exhales. "I don't know. Doc is being quiet about it near Calli, and I haven't wanted to interrupt him and Jaxx to get a full report. I think the baby is fine, the concern seems to be revolving around Calli."

"I'm sorry, majesty. I know how close the two of you are. Please tell me if there's anything I can do for either one of you."

Creed comes into the room, sees the state of his mate, and strides over to the opposite couch to sit with her. When he pulls her into his arms, she melts against his chest. "You're tired, Little Wolf. Let me take you upstairs for a rest."

Keyla snuggles closer and nuzzles into the side of his neck. "I'm fine here. If I doze off, leave me on the couch. I want to wake up and be there for Calli if anything happens."

"Wouldn't you be more comfortable in our bed?"

"Comfortable, yes, but I don't want to be that far with everything going on." She eases back and looks at her husband. "That reminds me, what *is* going on? Is the castle secure? Where's Rhy? Is he safe?"

Creed nods. "He's busily taking care of things in the security office. So far, our anti-insurgency measures have held up perfectly. The guards outside our door said there are a few hostiles within the castle but with the help of Hawk's men, Honor is conducting a full sweep to weed out any traitors in our midst."

I shift back on the seat of the sofa and adjust Moonshade in my lap. "I don't suppose Ruic Breard and his associates anticipated such strength in your defensive force at such short notice. You've done well, sire."

Creed waves that away. "It wasn't me. It was the foresight of Rhylan, Hawk, and Lukas that got us this far, and I have no doubt Honor will bring it full circle. She is coming into her own."

My chest warms with pride as he speaks the praises of my mates. While my strongest connection is with Lukas, my tender friendship and shared respect with Honor have bloomed into something I cherish and look forward to nurturing further.

"I know that look," Creed says, smiling at me. "That's mate pride if I've ever seen it."

"I am a blessed man to be included in their mating."

"You say that as if it's one-sided. They didn't include you out of pity. Honor and Lukas adore you. They recognize the same strength of character, compassion, and self-less charm we all see. You are a welcome member of our family."

"That is kind of you to say, sire. Gratitude."

Keyla's soft snore makes the two of us chuckle.

Creed leans back, adjusts his wife against his chest, and smiles over at me. "There's a blanket on the back of the sofa to your left. Do you mind tossing it over? I have a feeling this will be a long night. Might as well rest while we can."

I grab the blanket, shake it out of its folds, and stand to pass it. The shift in position demands I set Moonshade onto the floor and my vision of Creed and Keyla on the sofa is lost.

I hold the blanket out and release it when Creed accepts it. Moonshade is distracted and trots off without me. I call her back. I sense her reluctance to return at first but when she feels my sense of helplessness, she does as I ask.

"Gratitude, sweet girl." I scoop her up from the floor to shift her in my arms. "I sense your needs too. We can't go down onto the grounds right now, but I can take you into one of the walk-in showers to relieve yourself. They have tile floors and I'll rinse things off after. No one will know or be upset."

She finds that to be a good compromise and we take our leave. As King Creed said, it's going to be a long night and we need to take our moments while we can.

Lukas

I rise from the depths of unconsciousness with an incessant throbbing in the back of my skull and a persistent dread weighing on me. It takes a moment for my memory to catch up with my conscious mind and then it all comes back in a rush.

Infiltrating the barn... the bomb going off... being thrown

by the blast and watching as the enforcer beside me breathes his last breath.

"It was—" My voice cracks and I swallow against a parched throat. Not only is my throat dry, but my lungs feel tight from the smoke and my tongue is coated with the taste of creosote. "It was an ambush."

"It was." Tundra kneels at my side, a look of desperate horror etched on his face.

"What? Who died?"

He shakes his head. "I don't know how many. I found you next to one man but I have no idea about the others."

"What happened?"

"When I heard your voice over the comms, and you said you were in trouble, I flew in to extract you. By the time I found you and was able to lift us out of that fiery hell, the enemy had closed in. I didn't wait around, I brought you to safety to assess your injuries, and to ensure your survival."

I close my eyes and stretch, testing my muscles for any sign of pain and weakness. There is none. This isn't the first time I've woken up like this and there's only one treatment that leaves no residual of the original injury.

"You used phoenix tears on me."

"I did. You told me everyone within the inner circle carries a vial. I had nothing to offer you and you were suffering from catastrophic wounds. Removing the shrapnel from the bomb and using the tears to heal you was my only recourse."

He says it like he's apologizing but there's no way the guilt and agony he's hemorrhaging is because he used up a vial of phoenix tears.

"It's fine. The quint will lock Calli down with a couple of Romcoms and we'll have a fresh supply by the time the end credits are rolling. Don't worry about it."

But that's not it.

His gaze is haunted and the anger in them is unusual for him. "What's wrong, Tundra? What am I missing?"

He lifts one shoulder, and his wing adjusts and shuffles behind him. That powerful collection of feathers is usually snow white and pristine. Tonight, they are covered in ash and soot and singed with burns.

It pisses me off to see him like this. More than my anger from succumbing to my injuries. More than rebel assholes getting the upper hand on us. The look of self-recrimination on Tundra's face is too much.

"Talk to me, T. What's going on with you?"

"Men died tonight and it is my fault. I took the call from the tip line, and scanned the surroundings, and deemed the operation a go. Maybe I missed a cue that would have saved lives. In my haste to bring the guilty parties to justice, maybe I endangered the lives of you and your men."

I shake my head and close my eyes as the world spins. "You did no such thing. You took the tip, you presented it as an opportunity to close in on the rebels, and we all agreed it was a solid lead. There's no blame there, so stop beating yourself up."

My words make no difference. I'm not surprised. If the roles were reversed, and I didn't have the experience I do, I'd feel the same way.

"Tundra, if you face dangers long enough, you're going to lose men. It's never easy but it's a numbers game. It's pointless to beat yourself up. The only thing you can do is honor the fallen once we get back to our lives. Now, help me onto my feet."

He presses a gentle hand on my chest. "It's too soon. Even with the healing power of Calli's tears, you lost a lot of blood. I can see by the dilation of your pupils, you're still healing."

"Nah, I'm good."

"Is that so? Can you honestly tell me the world is not spinning around you?"

"It's no worse than a three-beer buzz."

"Except we're not going to a bonfire with friends. When we go back to that barn, we must be fighting fit. No offense, but you are far from that right now."

"You sound like Hawk."

"Thank you. From what I've seen, Hawk Barron is a strategic and intelligent man."

I chuckle and close my eyes. "Okay. I'll take another five minutes and see where we're at."

"You'll take an hour at least. Dawn is seducing the horizon. By that time, we'll be able to see what's coming at us. Breard's men knew we were coming and so knew what they would do once they captured us. Your men are either dead or captured already. Us rushing in to join them won't help anyone."

I hate that he's right but there's no arguing the point.

"Fine. One hour and not a minute more. The moment we can see what we're dealing with, we move out."

"Agreed."

I can't stand the look of failure in his eyes. "In the meantime, lay with me. I'm cold from the blood loss and need some body heat."

It's true enough to get him to comply.

The more important reason is to hold him and assuage his guilt. When he's settled, I reach over and pull him close. "If I have to rest and heal, so do you, mate."

CHAPTER TWO

Honor

*C*onnor MacDougal and I work through the night to oversee the lockdown of Thornebane Castle. As much as I admire his professionalism and knowledge, I wish a different FCO Tactical Squad Leader was at my side. Lukas has a way of getting things done, anticipating my needs, and putting me at ease at the same time.

He's a gifted male.

I check my watch to see if Tundra sent me any recent updates on their situation. A part of me has been holding my breath since his first report came in.

The tip was an ambush. Losses unknown. Casualties unknown. Evacuated Lukas to tend to his injuries. Situation dire. Will administer phoenix tears.

I've heard the tales of magical rejuvenation after receiving a dose of phoenix tears, but still... I worried.

The second came almost an hour later...

Lukas will recover. Resting until sunrise and will return to investigate the outcome of the raid.

Now, by the time on my watch, it must be almost time for the next update. Has Lukas made a full recovery? Are he and Tundra still good to regroup and try to find the others?

"Lady Thornebane." Connor closes the distance between the two of us in three long strides. "My men have detained two men they believe you might want to speak with. They were found trying to access a staircase towards the basement and refuse to answer any questions about what they were doing."

"If it's the staircase I'm thinking of, they were trying to access the security corridor."

"All the more reason to speak with them."

"Agreed."

The two of us strike off toward the security access stairs as the three other members of our team fall in behind us. The heels of my boots clack an angry rhythm against the marble floors as we make our way.

It's been a night.

At this moment, there's nothing I wouldn't give to be lounging in a hot bath with my mates safe, healthy, and joining me in a sexy soak.

My mind wanders, I'm going to need a much bigger bathtub. A hot tub, maybe. Yeah, I'll have to look into that. There are, of course, the soaking milk baths in the training center at Amberloq Hall but those offer no privacy. Eight sunken troughs in one large room hardly inspire intimate impulses.

When the five of us arrive at the steps leading down to the security floor, I'm pleased to see the door is still locked and, when I access the entry logs, no one has accessed or gone down since my exit hours ago.

"Excellent. All is well here. Take me to speak with the detainees."

"As ye wish, Princess. This way."

I follow Connor's lead, subtly turning my arm to check if Tundra sent me a message. My mind and body might be in this castle, but my heart and private thoughts are somewhere else entirely... with my mates.

Lukas

I wake from a fitful sleep, my mind filled with disjointed images of fire and failure. I check my watch, hoping Hawk checked in. He hasn't. That doesn't mean much. He could be a prisoner. He could have lost or damaged or had his watch removed. He could have his hands bound and not be able to send a message.

I activate the GPS tracking for him and the screen flips to a map. He's not close enough to where we were ambushed in that barn. He's much further.

That's a great sign.

I repeat the process, this time tracking Brant's signal. Same thing. Same place. That's very good news. If they were killed, why bother transporting the bodies across the quadrant? They wouldn't. They've been taken somewhere. The only other explanation would be if their watches were confiscated.

If that's the case, they might be dead, and we'll be tracking the men who did it. Not my favorite scenario, but I like the idea of finding the fuckers who attacked us.

The cave where Tundra brought me to recover faces the horizon of the rising sun. As beautiful as it is to see another day after facing my mortality, I tear my gaze from the golden glow rising in the distance to focus on something far more breathtaking.

Tundra's ebony brow is pinched tight with the stress of his night. Even lost in the grasp of exhaustion, he doesn't allow himself to rest.

He blames himself for the clusterfuck of the ambush. It's not his fault. He did what anyone would have and the result would've been the same.

And hey, he rescued me from a burning building, brought me here, and covered me with his own body to keep me warm while I healed.

That's heroic in my book.

Knowing we only have a few brief moments before we need to leave the sanctuary of this cave, I adjust my position, sending a wandering caress down the torn fabric of his T-shirt to the buckle of his belt.

With deft fingers, I release the pin of his belt and open up the two sides, giving me access to the fastener of his pants. My ministrations stir him from sleep and his muscled frame falls utterly still.

"This is your morning wake-up call," I say my voice graveled with sleep. "If you don't mind, I'd like to spend a quiet moment with my mate before we venture out into the hostile world again."

Tundra swallows, blinking as if I caught him in the middle of a dream. "Are you sure you're feeling well enough? It's only been a few hours."

I send the zipper down and open the front of his pants. His morning wood is thick and rigid, and now that I have access, I'm even more anxious to get at him.

"Good morning, mate." I lean in until our mouths fuse. There's something about almost dying that heightens life for the next while.

It's like that now with Tundra.

He tastes like smoke, but I don't care. There is only us. We went into hell together and we survived.

He saved my life.

Our tongues meet and the contact unlocks his reserve. His need is free and he comes at me with a groan and aggressive sweeps. He challenges me for dominance and I chuckle against his mouth unwilling to give him the right-of-way.

I've never taken a lover who is a fellow warrior.

This is new for me.

New is fun.

I'm getting distracted. My body responds to the kiss and makes demands of its own, but I intended to ease him and release some of his stress.

With my hand already accessing the opening of his pants, I slide my fingers under the elastic waistband of his boxers. I don't have to go far before I connect with the swollen crown of his cock. The tip is smooth and damp with the warm moisture of pre-cum.

I slide my thumb through the silky mess and play with the slit.

I break from our lip lock and tug his bottom lip with my teeth. When I let go, I'm jazzed to see the haunted worry that plagued him is gone, replaced by nothing but anticipation.

"We keep saying we're going to make time to be together, but I'll say it again. There is so much I want to spend time doing with you. This is just a morning sampler to start our day off right."

Before he has time to respond, I slide down his body and wriggle his pants lower to increase my access. The floor of the cave is hard and cool but relatively smooth. It's not the most comfortable place to get busy but it's also not the worst.

My lips part over his arousal.

"Oh, gods," he gasps, thrusting into my mouth.

I chuckle, settling in. This might be a quick fix but I'm serious about going to town and ramping both of us up higher. In my mind, I'm thanking him for saving my life. I'm telling him I think he's one hell of a warrior. I'm expressing how damned horny he makes me with those fucking wings of his.

If actions speak louder than words, I'm probably shouting from the rooftops right now.

Tundra's breathing is coming hard and fast.

He hooks his fingers at the back of my head on each side of my neck. Holding my mouth in place, he groans as he fucks my mouth, and I suck him off.

He's not the kind of man who loses control often. It's empowering to be able to bring him to such an honest state of pleasure.

I wish we had more time so we could fuck. I wish there was a camp roll or mattress under his ass instead of stone. I wish a lot of things were different but the most important thing is perfect.

He and I, like this, is perfect.

Reaching into the gap of fabric at the crux of his legs I cup his sac. His flesh is hot and smooth, and I play with his delicate orbs. I'm not a gentleman about it. I know how it feels to have someone twist and play a little rough with my balls.

Only another guy could know how good that feels.

How the electrical sensation of the connection sends zings of pleasure to the base of his cock and builds the pressure toward release.

How it pushes his limits, making him want to release so badly but knowing when he does, it's over so he holds back, fighting to hang on.

Bobbing my head up and down his shaft, I use my teeth to gently score his flesh. He groans, his hips rocking as he nears his end. His breath escapes in throaty gasps and then his hand locks on my head, holding me in place as he shatters.

Panting breaths rip from his throat as warm cum releases into my mouth. I hadn't thought about the differences in fae genetics, but Tundra's cream is unexpectedly sweet.

Something carnal in me revels in the taste. I drink him down, milking him, and sucking every ounce of his orgasm.

Swirling my tongue through the slit in his crown, I lap up every last drop.

As his breathing eases and his hips fall still, I swallow and raise my head. The suction of my hold on him releases with a pop and I grin, sure I've found the most delicious lollipop ever.

"So," I say, lowering myself onto my side next to him, "if it isn't clear yet, thank you for saving my life."

Tundra chuckles. "You're very welcome. Thank you for thanking me. I look forward to returning the favor."

I wipe a hand across my mouth and grin. Images of that take form in my head and now I'm looking forward to that too. "Something to daydream about on our travels today."

Tundra lifts his hips and pulls his underwear and pants back into place. Once he has his pants done up and his belt buckled, he rolls to his feet and steps towards the edge of the cave. "The sun is up. I guess that means it's time to go."

I get to my feet and join him, staring out at the landscape washed gold by the morning glow. "I need one more moment of your time."

Gripping his shoulder, I step in so we are chest to chest. After a strong hug, I ease back and give him one soft kiss. "Good morning. Let's make today a better day, shall we?"

Tundra nods. "Yes. Let's."

Honor

Connor Mac and I finish securing the castle by the time the sun starts to rise. I'm quickly running out of steam. It's been a long night. I'm tired. I'm worried about my mates. And it's been hours since I received the last update about Calli and her progress in delivering her baby. The last thing I heard was when her water broke.

"Hey, Rhy, how are we doing? Can we wrap this up and release the lockdown? We need to go outside and secure the grounds."

Rhylan glances up from the security console and he looks as bagged as I feel. "I think we can safely say the castle is secure. If you and the enforcers are ready to go outside, I can downgrade the lockdown and give you temporary access to the east door."

"Yeah, let's do that."

Rhylan picks up his tablet and swipes across the screen. When he's finished he gives me a thumbs up and points to my watch. "I sent a door code for you to use. It will unlock for five minutes. When you're ready to come back inside, text me and I'll send you another."

"You don't think we can call this a win?"

Rhy shakes his head. "Not while there are a hundred rebels out there, no. Once they're secured, I'll consider it, but not before."

"He's got a fair point, lass," Mac says, his deep red curls swaying as he nods his head. "The job isn't finished until it's complete."

"That's profound, Mac."

"I thought so."

"Oh, Rhylan, sorry, this is Connor MacDougall, one of Hawk's men."

"Thanks for all your help," he says. "You and your men came through for us."

"Och, it's our pleasure to serve. And aside from a couple of run-ins with a citizen and two staff members caught trying to force their way through the new security door, it was pretty uneventful."

"Inside at least." Rhy flips the viewing of the monitor wall so images of the downed soldiers scattered all over the castle grounds fill the screens. I suppose we have to go outside to start cleaning up the grass. I figure the landscapers will protest if we leave them there."

"Can we mow over them?" I ask.

"We could, but we already have to go out and clean up the spider sentinels. Might as well multitask."

I chuckle. "Yeah, I suppose we don't want to leave them running around wild out there."

Rhylan lifts his handheld tablet and slides his finger over the glossy screen. "Tell me more about the two trying to get through the security door. What was that?"

"Not sure. My best guess is they didn't realize that door was installed and thought they'd have a clear shot at getting down here. Connor's men isolated them and a couple of other offenders in the cafeteria. Now that we're pretty sure the raid is over, I'll have the troublemakers escorted to the prison cells for interrogation."

"Are we handling that as well?" Connor asks.

"No, I'd prefer if Rhylan takes care of that later. We need to get control of those rebels before the tranq darts wear off."

Rhylan nods. "Once we finish with clean up, I'll catch a few hours of sleep somewhere and get to that."

"Yeah, you and me both. It seems we've both been displaced from our beds. The King's Tower won't become accessible for another ten or eleven hours and Amberloq Hall is overrun by the rebels who fled from the sentinels."

Rhylan's eyes widened at that. "How did you find that out?"

"Dune checked in ten minutes ago. He arrived back last night during the chaos and when he couldn't get into the castle, he went to Amberloq Hall. He was in the security panic room below the oculus window for most of the night. He said he tried to get in touch with us but all communications have been jammed. This morning he used his tactical watch to text me."

Rhylan lets off a long exhale. "So, communications are still jammed, Amberloq Hall is under the control of goblins, and we haven't heard back from the scouting party since they were ambushed."

"That sounds about right."

"Why do I get the feeling this raid isn't as over as we'd like it to be?"

That's not what I want to hear but is not wrong.

There are still definite issues to face before we can say we're in the clear. "First things first, we need to round up the assholes littering the lawn. Since the frequency of tactical watches isn't being jammed, we'll use them to communicate until we find the jamming device."

"All right. And where are you thinking for the holding area for the prisoners? There are hundreds of men out there. We don't have any facility large enough to house that many people."

"I've been thinking about that. I suggest we deescalate. We don't want to make enemies out of the citizens. The men out there are husbands and sons and brothers of families in Dornte. We should treat them with the respect we would any citizen. We need to show them why they are wrong in thinking Ruic Breard is the man they want to follow."

"How do ye plan to do that, lass?" Mac asks.

"We'll interrogate them, take down their personal information, and place them under a provisional release program. They can go to work, go home, and that's it. Laryssa was the queen of tracking chips and invasion of privacy. We'll take a page out of her book and keep a tight leash on these people."

"Chip them? Doesn't that make us as bad as Laryssa and her entourage?" Rhylan asks.

"Yes and no. We're offering them a chance to continue to provide for their family instead of going to jail. We'll make it clear that once we defeat Ruic Breard and his followers, the chips will be removed and their error in judgment pardoned."

"Pardoned? Seriously?"

I nod. "Yeah, seriously. What did they actually do? They

jumped out of a truck and ran across the public lawn of the castle. We'll never be able to prove intent."

Rhylan barks a laugh. "So, it's a case of me and my closest two-hundred friends just decided to dress in black, hide in the back of a semi-truck, and take a jog across the castle lawn for the hell of it?"

"Something like that." I wave away the look of his disapproval. "These men still have a chance to turn this around and we're going to be generous enough to give them that chance."

"And if they go running straight back to Ruic?"

"We'll make it clear, if anyone who rose against the Thornebane rule tonight is found participating in a second assault on the quadrant, they'll lose the privilege of their provisional arrest and will be imprisoned like a common criminal."

Rhylan rubs a hand across his jaw and covers a yawn. "I'm too tired to argue. Wouldn't it just be easier to line them up and shoot them?"

I chuckle. "Easier maybe but not better for Creed's rule. I'll take the FCO reinforcements out to round up the prisoners. You're in charge of finding the tracking equipment and getting us set up for the debriefing."

Rhylan shrugs. "Consider it done. I hope you're right about this. I'd hate for this to come back and bite us in the ass."

I back away from the conversation and head toward the door. "Don't worry. It'll be fine. What's the worst that could happen?"

Rhylan barks a laugh. "You kill me when you say shit like that."

CHAPTER THREE

Dune

By six o'clock in the morning, my ass is numb from sitting on the floor of the oculus room and my eyes are about to bleed from reading a mind-numbing manual for the past hours. The good news is, I think I have a handle on how these tactical watches work.

With that in mind, I click the second button with my left thumb and scroll the outer ring of the face until a blank screen pops up. After tapping it once, I press my finger on the keypad and start swiping my message.

In the oculus room of Amberloq Hall. The place is crawling with goblin assholes. Communication channels are jammed. Please advise.

I re-read my message and decide that pretty much covers it. When I hit the send button, an empty box appears in front of my message awaiting a recipient. Thankfully all of our watches have been programmed with the contact information we need.

Rhylan Silverwing is a damn good man to have on your team in a jam.

I select Honor's name from the list of contacts and hit send.

While I wait for a reply, I force myself to get up, curse the pins and needles in my legs, and hope that when Honor's reply comes, her orders involve me getting out of this cylindrical cone of solitude.

Dune! So happy to hear from you. The castle attack is under control. Activate your tracker for Lukas and Tundra. They left on a mission and were ambushed. Provide backup and bring them home.

Tundra went out on a mission and it failed? That thought sends eels squirming through my intestines.

Despite me not being Lukas's biggest fan, the guy is rock solid on military strategy and execution. It's hard to imagine him getting ambushed by anything or anyone. It must've been one hell of a fight.

Grabbing my tablet off the floor, I limp over to the security console and set it in front of me as my legs continue to torture me with pins and needles.

Calling up the section on activating GPS tracking, I hold my watch up so I can see it and start the process. I remember reading the part about how to locate another signal within my contacts but not what it said.

Groaning, I open the files on my tablet again and get back to studying. The moment I have a location for Tundra, I will unlock the glass window of the oculus room and launch skyward.

Unfortunately... it might take a minute

"I'm coming Iceman. Coming to back up that lovely ass of yours yet again... as soon as I find you."

Tundra

My skin is still tingling from the morning wake-up session with Lukas when the two of us leave the cave. I was worried we'd be

27

late to get started but we're right on schedule. The sun is only now fully rising, and the improved visibility will allow us to better prepare for what we're about to face.

"Back to the barn, or back to the helicopter?" I ask.

Lukas is staring out at the desolate terrain stretching before us and frowns. "I'm concerned about returning to the helicopter. Breard's men knew we were coming. We have to assume the helicopter was compromised and they are there waiting for us."

"I considered that."

"So, the question then becomes how far will we have to travel to find Hawk and Brant? At least with the helicopter, I'm able to cover long distances with you. Without it, we're on foot or stealing a vehicle."

"I'm capable of carrying you in flight."

"For short distances, sure, but from what I can tell from the coordinates, our men have been taken several hours away. That's too far for you to have to piggyback me all the way."

"First, it's *not* too far. I can do it. Second, it wouldn't be piggyback. I'd carry you cradled in my arms like a baby."

The look of indignation on Lukas's face is too funny. "Fuck you, Iceman."

There's no holding back my laughter. I bend over, patting my stomach as the pressure of the situation lessens at the expense of my mate.

Lukas punches me in the shoulder and laughs himself. "You're an asshole. I didn't know you even had a sense of humor, T."

"I do. I just save it for special occasions."

Lukas chuckles. "Lucky me."

I smile for a moment more and then circle back to the point of our conversation. "There's no way Breard's men missed me flying out of the fire last night. The fact that they didn't come after us surprised me. Either we didn't matter enough to them to come looking, or they figure they'll get us another way."

"It was a hectic scene. Is there's a chance they didn't see you?"

I lift a shoulder. "Likely not. They were firing blasters at me the whole time."

Lukas scowls out at the terrain laid out in front of us. "Back to the transportation issue. I say we hoof it for a few miles in the direction of the signal for Hawk and Brant. Then you fly me to the nearest town to rent a car."

"A few miles in the direction of the coordinates puts us on a path toward the helicopter. I say we get close and then I'll swoop in and see if it's compromised. Maybe they didn't care about that either. Or maybe they don't even know what a helicopter is."

"Do you think that's possible?"

"It's possible. Other than us and the Travon dragons, no one else has ever seen a helicopter before. Goblins aren't the smartest race. They might be afraid of the scary metal bird and fled the scene."

Lukas doesn't look convinced, but we've got a bit of hiking time to think about it.

Honor

Connor Mac and I take all but a few of the FCO enforcers and head out to detain the rebels and clean up the grounds. Rhylan disengaged the sentinel spiders before we came outside and they now sit eerily still, littered everywhere on the grass.

Creepsville.

I sweep a gesture toward the acres of grass. "I need several of you to gather those spiders and set them in one place for reinsertion. Those are Mr. Barron's pet projects, so be careful with them."

Four enforcers raise their hands and Mac gives them a nod. "The rest of ye are on garbage duty."

It takes a moment to catch up with that one. "Because we're taking out the trash?"

"Exactly, lass. If these green-skinned, wonky-nosed bastards don't recognize the difference between a ruler who cares for the people and a ruler who wants to make the rich richer, they're little more than trash on the street in my opinion."

I'm glad he said it because I can't.

As a member of the royal family, voicing opinions like that is bound to get me into hot water. There is enough chaos in the quadrant right now without adding kerosene to the fire.

Standing in the middle of the aftermath, it's hard not to think about how much worse it could have been.

If Rhylan hadn't locked down the castle as quickly as he did...

If Creed hadn't considered the extra safety measures of putting metal screens on all the windows...

If Hawk hadn't established the sentinel spiders and the bolsters to stop traffic at the entrance gate...

This could have been a very dark morning.

"Slecking bitch," a long-nosed goblin snaps at me as he's pulled to his feet. "You're living your last days of privilege, little princess. The people are tired of your family sitting in this castle looking down on us."

He's taunting me. I shouldn't take the bait... but I've never been good at turning a deaf ear. "Oh, from what I've heard, Thornebane popularity has never been higher. The people know Creed and I care about the quadrant and protecting the voice of the people."

"You just don't want to lose the life of luxury. You don't care about us. You know nothing about what it's like to live and work in this quadrant."

Rude. "I don't? I'm not sure whose version of history you're listening to. If you knew anything about the Thornebanes and the way my father ruled, you'd know both Creed and I were sent into the workforce at the age of fourteen."

"The workforce?" another goblin shouts. "It doesn't count as work if daddy gets you the cushy jobs so you can look good but keep your hands clean."

I laugh out loud. "Yeah, I looked amazing while I cleaned toilets at the portal hub. Even better when I was wearing those stupid plastic visors they make you wear at the quadrant conveyance office. Yeah, I rocked that look for a year as I processed public credits and vehicle licenses."

"Do you expect us to believe that?"

"Believe what you want. It's a matter of public record. All municipal workers are listed in the personnel files. You're free to access my work history in the town hall records room."

"Anybody could've listed you there."

"Then look up anyone who worked there at the same time and ask them."

"I don't care that much."

I shrug. "That's fair. I'm just saying, I may live in a castle on a hill overlooking the city, but that just meant I had to set my alarm earlier in the morning to catch a public shuttle to get to work on time."

"Why are you still talking?" a fat goblin with a bad case of whispy comeover asks. "Are your feelings hurt, little girl?"

"Hardly. I don't give two shits if you judge me but I'd prefer it if your opinion was based on truth and not propaganda fed to you by Ruic Breard."

Longnose guy grunts. "He said you would turn this around on him and play the victim."

Rage fires in my cells and I straighten to my full height and release my wings.

"I'm no one's victim. Yes, my parents were slaughtered right in front of me, and I was raped repeatedly at Laryssa's order, and then tortured by the Blood Witch. That's not who I am, that's a list of horrible events that happened to me. I'm much more."

"Not from where I'm standing," the fat one says. "I see a silver-haired bitch who is out of touch with the quadrant and doesn't care what the citizens need."

I laugh. "You might want to reconsider that, fatty. I'm the one who stood up for all of you and said we should give you a second chance. I voted to send you all home to your families with a warning on a conditional release. But by all means, if you'd rather be jailed and tried for conspiring against the crown, go ahead. I'll change my mind."

"No!" A skinny man with lopsided ears pierces me with a pleading gaze. Mac has him on his feet and is passing him off to another soldier. "My wife will kill me if I get arrested. I told her I was picking up a shift in Travon. If forgiveness is possible, I vote for that."

Fatty fights against the soldier holding him and twists to glare. "You're afraid of your wife?"

"I am. If you aren't, you're stupider than you look."

The two lunge toward each other but with their hands bound and the paralysis still in effect, they don't get far. They mostly tip awkwardly toward each other and faceplant in the grass.

I laugh, turning toward Mac to get this lawn cleanup moving. I'm tired and I want my bed—

An ear-shattering explosion *cracks* behind me.

I duck and spin.

An electrified net rains down over us.

I lunge forward, trying to get clear of the fallout but

someone grabs my leg and drags me to the ground. I'm yanked backward and then the weight of the net hits.

"Ow, shit!" Anywhere I've got exposed skin, the netting snaps hot against my flesh. My wings and lower back sizzle and I flail and flip to stop the burn.

A thundering roar of footsteps approaches and I swing my legs to drag myself around to see what's coming. Crap. Raiders coming in from the forest path.

"It's the assholes who hid in Amberloq Hall."

Dammit. I figured we could get these rebels under control before we faced a battle on two fronts.

Blaster fire sounds and at the same time gunshots are firing from an automatic weapon. *Tat-a-tat-a-tat.*

We're sitting ducks—no, I guess we're more like rabbits snared in a net.

"Get this motherfuckin' net off of me," Mac shouts, close to my left. At least I think it's him. He's been one hundred percent unflappable since this all began. Now, he's seriously losing his shit. "I need this net off me!"

I scramble toward his voice, army-crawling on the manicured grass. With each pull forward, the netting hooks and singes my wings. It sends a rush of nausea through me. If I'd eaten anything today, I'd be puking. As it is, I'm fighting to not pass out.

"Mac?" I reach forward and place a hand on his powerful leg. "Mac, are you okay?"

His pants split beneath my hand and I pull it back when I feel the fur beneath.

WTF?

Right. I know nothing about the man. He is obviously a wildling or shifter of some kind. Hopefully, he's sentient in his animal form because I'm right beside him and will be the first delectable morsel he encounters when he gets his claws and teeth.

Tat-a-tat-a-tat.

Dammit. Mac's right. We need to get out from under this net. Rolling onto my back, I grab the mesh and start pulling. It has an end, so that means if I keep pulling, I'll find it. The moment my fingers tighten around the mesh, electrical energy stings my fingers and courses up my arms.

I bite my lip to keep from crying out but that doesn't keep hot tears from streaming down my cheeks.

Focused as I am on getting free, I miss the end of Mac's transformation... that is until he stands on all fours beside me. "Holy shit."

Lying on my back, I'm staring up at a massive red cat... and by massive, I mean a cat the size of a horse. He's shaggy and tall and when he growls, it rumbles in my chest like there's a vibrating speaker beneath my ribs. I've never seen anything like him.

Tat-a-tat-a-tat.

Right. Admire the giant kitty later.

Mac's powerful frame lifted the net so far off the ground I can stand and help pull it off us. The moment I free him, he gives me a look of thanks and then his claws find purchase. He sends chunks of grass and dirt into the air as he runs at the enemy, fangs bared.

I hope they wore their brown boxers because... yeah, I bet they're shitting themselves.

Tat-a-tat-a-tat.

An excruciating burn explodes in my arm.

I scream, twisting away from the strike and trying to see— oh good. There's a graze across my shoulder but it's not bad.

Pulling my blaster, I assess the attackers and glance around for cover. There is none. I'm standing in the middle of a vast back lawn of a castle. The only thing around us is other bodies ducking away from being hit.

Some of the prisoners released from their paralysis are

emboldened by the attack. They're up and fighting. Fatty takes a run at me and lowers his shoulder to use as a body ram.

Seriously? Does he think he can overpower me in a melee fight with his hands bound? Not bloody likely.

I wait for him to get close and then I blast him with my setting on stun. His eyes bug out and he looks at me dazed and confused. Hilarious. "Yeah, I'm holding a blaster, dumbass. Did you miss that part?"

There's no time to enjoy the moment because shooters are closing in. With no other option, I grab fatty and use him as a shield. His fellow rebels don't seem worried about their comrade-in-arms because they're firing on us without end.

I tuck in closer to fatty's back but now that he's been swiss-cheesed, he's sinking toward the ground and I'm losing my shield.

I can't hold my blaster and him too. I have to choose. It's a shitty either-or. Either I have no weapon to defend myself or I have no shield to defend myself.

Augh! I drop my blaster and use both hands to hold fatty up in front of me. Hopefully, when the incoming attackers get close enough, I'll be able to jump out from behind him and fight my way free.

A shadow passes overhead.

I curse, ducking and ready for an attack from above.

Mac the giant cat roars from the other side of the lawn but there's no way he can get to me in time. I twist, staring up into the sky but the sun is directly in my eyes and I can't see.

There's nothing to be done about that.

Refocusing on the forces coming at me, I brace for impact. Dammit, there are five of them. This is going to hurt. I adjust my stance to brace myself but they hit like a freight train.

I'm knocked back and my brain is rattled...

I've got no time to nurse my wounds. I try to scramble to my feet but Fatty's body fell across my legs. I kick, trying to gain my freedom.

Punches are coming at me.

Pinned to the ground, there's nothing else to do but curl up and protect myself the best I can.

The pain from the first few hits echos in my body. I want to fight. I'm still kicking at the weight pinning my legs when the punches raining down on me stop.

I take the opportunity to reach down but Fatty's body gets flung off my legs and I'm free. Rolling to my feet, I pull in a lungful of air and scramble to get moving again.

Tat-a-tat-a-tat.

A solid weight forces me to the ground and someone drops to the ground and curls around me. I'm crouched in a battered and bleeding ball and it takes a moment to recognize the arms embracing me. And the sandy brown feathers that are so reminiscent of a falcon.

Dune's here. "Hey, Sandman."

"Hello, beautiful," he says, close to my ear. "How's your day going, honey?"

I half laugh and half choke. "I've had better."

"I bet. Five on one with no weapon isn't good."

I close my eyes and let the comfort of Dune's arms transport me from this hell. I know it's only for a moment, but I'll take it.

"Has the shooting stopped?" I twist my gaze to the side and glance back. The shift in position brings my mouth to within an inch of his. "Hey there."

He winks, his smile soft and intimate. "Hey there."

Closing the distance, he places a warm kiss on the end of my nose. It's sweet and honest and exactly right. "And to answer your question, yes, I think that big red cat chew-toyed the bad guys. We're good."

CHAPTER FOUR

Lukas

$\mathcal{I}$t takes us less than an hour to hike back to where I landed the helicopter. During that time, Tundra convinces me to at least investigate whether or not the goblins have secured our best option.

Either I'm getting soft in my old age, or this mating thing is melting my iron will. Honestly, hopping into the cockpit and flying is by far the more enticing answer to our transportation problem.

By tracking the location on my watch, the two of us stop just short of the ridge overlooking the clearing. "I placed a mist of confusion spell on the helicopter when I left, but I still think they likely found it."

"As I said before, goblins aren't the smartest race. They are greedy and cutthroat but lack the brainpower to impress the world with their intelligence."

"Ruic Breard seems to be smart enough. He's got the entire quadrant in a tizzy and has managed to pull together a decent rebellion against the Thornebanes."

"That's because his interests are money-based. Goblins know about currency and gold and economic pressures. Something like a mist of confusion spell surrounding a mode of transportation they don't understand will have them baffled."

"I'll take your word for it but if we get down there and get our asses kicked, I'm holding you responsible."

He doesn't seem concerned. "The good news is if we do get our asses kicked and we are taken prisoner, they might take us to where they're holding Brant and Hawk. Then we won't have to lift a finger to find them."

I cast a sidelong glance and laugh. "That's what you're going with?"

Tundra laughs. Despite it being nice to see him as comfortable as he is, I wonder why... especially considering the situation.

"What changed with you?" I ask. "You seem a lot more relaxed than usual."

He lifts one shoulder in a shrug. "Last night we almost died. I watched you lying there for hours, worrying. I was worried about Honor and the raiders at the castle. I worried about Dune and wondered where he is and why he hasn't returned."

"It's been a hell of a couple of days, that's for sure."

"It has, indeed. Then this morning I woke up and you were healthy and well and seduced me."

I laugh. "No apologies."

"None needed. It's just after the stress of last night, all of that lifted. You're alive and well, Honor sent word they held the castle and are fine, and there's a good chance Hawk, Brant, and your men survived the ambush and are merely being held as prisoners."

"It's a good day to be alive."

"It is."

"Also, for the first time in my life, I feel like I'm not on my own. We may be the underdogs battling against men with more money than sense with no Amberloq force and no idea what's going to happen, but you're here with me and that's enough. Whatever happens, we'll face it together."

I raise my arm, clasp hands with him, and tug him forward so we are chest to chest. "Damn straight. We've got this. Whatever happens, it's you and me, T. Our lives together are just beginning, and I see great things in our future."

Tundra grins. "I'm looking forward to it. So, how about we go get our asses kicked and reclaim your helicopter?"

"Sounds good to me."

～

Shadow

"Moonshade, sweet girl, remember to focus." I pull my hands back from the stove until my little wolf gives me her attention back. With my finger, I tap on the counter of the kitchen island to get her to look at me. "If you want me to cook you up some yummy ham and eggs, you need to watch the pan so I can see what I'm doing."

It sounds silly to be convincing a wolf to focus but even though it's been less than a day, the two of us have made remarkable strides.

She's incredibly smart and intuitive.

She also wants to please me.

I doubt she could do anything *but* please me. Her distraction isn't her fault. First and foremost, she's a wolf and yearns to be out in nature. We've been cooped up in the King's Tower for over twelve hours. No fresh air rustling in her fur. No stretching her legs on the castle lawn. No scents to follow in the long grasses and treed forest of the grounds.

"It won't be long now, little one. Honor texted us that the bad guys outside are being rounded up and the castle is no longer in danger. Once that's taken care of, we will be able to go out and explore the forest."

I sense the surge of excitement within her as images start playing in my mind. A wild creature, Moonshade doesn't speak to me in words but rather in impressions and pictures of the world.

Right now, she is showing me images of her racing through the trees of the forest, tucking under low-draping foliage, and digging in the pithy soil.

"Is that your plan when the lockdown is lifted?"

That's a definite yes.

I grin and reclaim my spatula. "Then let's finish with breakfast and be ready for when the metal screens rise and we're free to go outside."

Moonshade focuses on watching me cook, so I can finish. The sooner we eat, the sooner we can get outside. I'm hoping a little food and fresh air will help with the headache that's looming behind my eyes.

I'm not sure if it's an aftereffect of hitting my head in the car accident or of my maternal genes activating, but I've had more headaches in the past week than I have my entire life.

"Somethin' smells good in here." Jaxx joins us in the kitchen and heads straight to the coffee maker. The Jaguar looks like he hasn't slept in a week, and maybe that's true.

Keyla mentioned that of all the males in the Phoenix Quint, Jaxx is the one most worried about the baby and its mother.

"There's plenty if you're hungry."

"I'm famished, actually, but I don't know that my stomach will accept food at the moment. I better stick with coffee for now."

"What if I made something a little easier on your digestion? You must keep up your strength for Calli."

The mention of his mate triggers a look of worry and sorrow.

"I am sorry she is struggling through this delivery. You and Kotah are here for her and Doc and Keyla are dedicated to ensuring everything turns out as it's meant to. Try not to worry."

"Try not to worry? There hasn't been a phoenix birth in a millennium. There's no information on what we need to do. Doc and I have no clue if we've got a handle on it. For all I know, we're screwin' up and will kill my mate and my cub. Try not to worry? That's pretty fuckin' stupid advice, Counsellor."

The anger in Jaxx's voice draws Moonshade's attention. She turns her attention on him and I not only feel how unsettled she is, I see why.

Jaxx's fingers are curled into fists, his body shaking as the low rumble of his cat's fury fills the space.

Moonshade growls right back, her need to protect me rising to the fore. "My sincerest apologies, Jaxx. I meant only to comfort you in a difficult time. Forgive my insensitivity."

I've pretty much finished cooking our breakfast, so I find the dial for the burner and shut things off. Turning away from the stove, I reach one hand into the air, searching for the doorknob of the cabinet.

Thankfully, when I woke from my coma a few weeks ago, I spent enough time in this kitchen I have a sense of where things are even without my sight. I managed to find and open the cabinet door for the plates and reach in to get myself set up for breakfast.

The shuffle of ceramic draws Moonshade's attention to what I'm doing and then I see myself and get our meal dished up.

"No, Shadow," Jaxx says, his voice deep. "I'm tired and stressed and not fit company. You don't need to apologize to me. It's me who needs to apologize to you."

"Your reaction was perfectly understandable. I didn't mean to upset you more than you already are."

I set my plate on the counter in front of Moonshade and it's amazing how focused she is now. I doubt I'll have trouble cutting up my meals with her around because she's very interested in what's on my plate.

"Shadow? That premonition you had... Did you get anything more on that since the other day?"

The premonition he's asking about is not a premonition at all. It was the first prophecy I made since my transition to an Oracle.

The child of fire, the moon of light,
A sea of blood to stain the night,
The foe of freedom, the king is down,
A war of outcasts to hold the crown.

"Well, we all agreed the child of fire is your young, and the moon of light means something will happen under the full moon. Depending on which of the moons of Dornte are being referenced, whatever is pending won't happen for another week or two. That leads me to believe everything will turn out fine with the birthing."

I can't see Jaxx's reaction because Moonshade is still hyperfocused on the ham and eggs, but his breathing is slowing down.

"Thanks, Shadow. That makes sense. Why do you think our cub was mentioned at all? Will she be involved in this somehow? Should we leave the realm and go home to keep her out of danger?"

"I wondered about that. The rebellion seems to have ended before it began last night. The king did not fall, and no blood was shed. Either that means the prophecy wasn't realized or the mention of the baby being born is the first sign of the prophecy and the events don't all happen at once."

"So, more like a list of what's to come? First, the birth of the baby, then bloodshed, the fall of the king, and then the army of outcasts turn the tides so Creed can hold the crown."

"That's one possible way to interpret it, yes."

Jaxx squeezes my shoulder. "All right then, I can live with that. It means we have a troubled time on the horizon, but everything works out. I can get behind that."

Jaxx leaves Moonshade and me alone to share our breakfast and I send Calli and her mates as much healing energy as I can manage.

Yes, I may have lost my sight and my place in Elven society and be on a rocky path of my own, but I have my health, my place with Lukas and Honor and their mates, and now I have Moonshade. With all the turmoil and heartbreak surrounding me, I won't lose sight of the fact that I remain blessed.

~

Tundra

Lukas and I spread out as we approach the small clearing where he landed the helicopter last night. We take time to survey the area and find two goblins wandering the perimeter of the clearing and another four heavily armed men playing a game of kradnic bones in the dirt by the tail rotor of the metal bird.

From what Lukas says, they are probably aware there is something important they are supposed to do, but the mist of confusion makes it so they can't focus enough to know for sure what that is.

The magic he possesses is awe-inspiring.

With him being born and raised in the other realm, I've never met anyone with his unique skill set. Explicit images invade my focus and I'm momentarily pulled back into that cave with his mouth around my cock.

That's another awe-inspiring skill he possesses.

I smile at how quickly my body responds.

Before being sent to Mount Hekko with Dune, I never

considered having a sexual relationship with another man. It's amazing how the world opens when you're removed from your everyday options.

I make my way around an upturned tree, ducking behind the unearthed roots. The shift in position allows me a visual of the helicopter and its guards.

Dune and I are a textbook case of opposites attract.

No, that's not correct... We are much more like enemies to lovers. That man gets under my skin and pisses me off more than anyone else alive.

And still, I can't get enough of him.

I've tried to walk away from him and deny what the two of us do with each other, but it's no use. At some point during those two years, we were stranded and forgotten on that mountain, we became more than a sexual outlet for one another.

We became lovers.

I'm not sure I would admit that to him—at least not yet. He has a lot of growing up to do first.

A high-pitched bird song floats upon the breeze and I refocus on the helicopter. Lukas told me to listen for his signal.

He's moving in.

There's no way for the two of us to get to the helicopter, get him inside, and give him the time to start things up without drawing the attention of the six goblins here to guard it.

The plan is to knock out as many as we can in a quick melee fight and then for me to take on as many as I can while he fires up the engines and gets ready to fly.

The fighting part is fine with me, I have a lot of pent-up anger about the ambush last night. No matter what Lukas says to the contrary, I carry the weight of this fiasco on my shoulders.

The only way I can appease that guilt is to ensure we rescue all the survivors.

That won't bring back the men who are dead. For them, I

fight. For Hawk and Brant, I fight. And for the annihilation of the Elbirfae communities, I fight.

Adrenaline burns hot in my blood as I launch out from behind the screen of the tree roots and target the two men working the perimeter.

Goblins may not be the smartest race, but they have quick reflexes and are dirty fighters. The two men I approach turn with surprise in their jaundice yellow eyes and raise their weapons.

I'm in striking distance before they have a chance to fire. With a hard backfist, I catch the first man in the jaw and swing his head around like an owl.

At the same time, I thrust my wing open and catch the second man across the chest. The impact knocks him off his feet and into a patch of boulders on the ground. His body falls in an awkward tangle and a loud crack rings out as his head connects with the ground.

I didn't mean for him to crack his head on the stone, but I feel no guilt over it.

Some things in war can't be avoided.

The scuffle with these two draws the attention of the other four. The men abandon their game of bones and are on their feet and rushing me.

An orb of blue magic takes one man to the ground, and I feel the power of Lukas's gifts raise the hair on my scalp. Somehow, I recognize the signature of the energy as being part of him. I'm not sure how that works, but there's no question in my mind.

I feel him in that magic.

The other three are upon me and I get ready for battle. Three goblin rebels against one Amberloq General is hardly fair. They are no more threatening to me than junior sparring partners.

"Are you good, T?" Lukas asks.

"Fine. Get your bird off the ground."

Lukas laughs, jogging toward the cockpit of the helicopter. "Are you coming on to me, Iceman?"

I raise my arm to block an incoming fist and play my words back in my mind... Oh, get his bird off the ground. I chuckle, sweeping my wing and knocking two men into each other. "I wasn't, but I am now."

Lukas continues to laugh as he presses the keypad and unlocks the door of the chopper. Once he's inside, he's busy with the switches and dials he needs to get mobile. Focused as he is, he misses the arrival of six more rebel fighters.

Two of them are goblins, but the other four come from tougher stock—dwarves if I had to guess. I'm now pitted against nine opponents and am forced to rethink my position in this fight.

I can't win this.

All I need to do is hold my own until Lukas takes off and then we'll both be airborne.

A laser bolt shoots past my cheek and singes my skin. I spin away from the burn and call forward my shielding. My natural armor will protect me from laser blasts, but these odds present different dangers.

Lukas raises his head to put on his helmet and notices my situation. By the shift in his position, he's about to get out to join the fight.

I wave him off. He needs to get that helicopter in the air so we can get out of here.

We need to follow the tracking and get Brant and Hawk and the others to safety.

My fists are flying, and my wings are sweeping in frantic thrusts to keep my opponents at a distance. At the same time, my feathered appendages are shielding me from incoming laser blasts.

It's no use.

Three of them charge and take me to the ground.

A strong fist connects with my eye and knocks my face to the side as if my head is on a swivel. Pain explodes in the bone of my cheek and my eyes sting as it begins to water.

I raise my elbow to protect my face, punching with my free hand to keep my enemy from getting another shot. Getting knocked out by dwarfs would be bad. I try to roll to my side to get my wing far enough over me to act as a shield.

Slecking hell, there are so many of them.

Until there aren't.

From one moment to the next the weight pinning me down is gone. The sound of the rotors spinning grows louder and stronger and for that I'm grateful.

If Lukas was able to jump out and give me a moment's reprieve from the beating, I'm certainly not going to waste the opportunity.

I roll to my feet and gather myself and continue to fight, except it's not Lukas who came to my aid...

As fists fly and men are knocked back on their asses, it's Dune who smiles over at me and winks. The flutter in my chest is neither professional nor manly but I refuse to look at it too closely.

He's here and he's saving my ass.

"Good to see you, Dune. I'm so pleased you could join the fun."

Dune spins with his right wing fully extended. The radius of his reach clotheslines two goblins and he knocks them flying into the dirt. "Fun you say? It looked to me like you are getting your ass kicked. Then again, you always liked it a little rough."

The sexual tone of the teasing is new. Usually, when Dune mouths off he is just a dick. I'm not sure I enjoy sharing our personal life with the enemy but considering how worried I've been about his safety and peace of mind the past two days, I'm happy to overlook it.

The thrumming beat of the helicopter rotors grows faster in

its rhythm. I duck a little raising my hand to shield my eyes from the sand and debris swirling in the air. As the wheels of the helicopter lift off the ground, my focus shifts from fight to flight.

Lukas navigates the mechanical bird into the air with a grace I still don't understand, but I don't have to. The point of it is, he's in the air and lifting into the sky so Dune and I are free to join him.

"Feel like getting out of here?" I ask.

Dune shrugs. "This is your party. I'm just crashing."

I crouch for a moment before pushing upward to launch into the air. As I pump my wings and gain elevation, I smile to myself.

This is the Dune I could learn to love... the playful, easygoing warrior ready for a fight.

If only he could be this male more often.

CHAPTER FIVE

Honor

onnor Mac and I spent a good part of the rest of the day on the lawn with his officers. The second strike made an even bigger mess of things and, though I'd never say this out loud, the giant Mac cat is a very messy killer. The horror scene does work to our advantage though. The rebels who aren't dead have gone silent and are being very agreeable while we take them into custody.

It's after lunch by the time the manicured grounds of Thornebane Castle are no longer littered with the bodies.

"That looks better, don't you think?"

Mac tilts his head from side to side, his long russet curls swaying in the summer breeze. "Better than the bloody death, for sure. Although, the scattered ninja look was kind of funny. I don't condone it, but more than a few of my men took pictures."

I chuckle, scanning for anything or anyone we might have missed. "I don't hold that against them. I may have taken a couple myself."

"So, what now, Princess?"

"Now we take this last group to Rhylan to be processed and then send a group of your enforcers to sweep Amberloq Hall and ensure there aren't any raiders still there from the ones who fled the sentinels last night."

"It was good of ye to put them up for the night."

"Like I had any choice. Hopefully, they've all fled by now, but if they're still there, I want them out."

Connor turns to the closest members of his crew and nods. "Ye heard the lady. Wrap up the last of our presents fer the dragon, round up a squadron, and ready to evict the last of the squatters if they're dumb enough to still be hidin' out."

"Yes, sir," a couple of the men say.

"Oh, and give the place a quick bomb and bug sweep too."

"Yes, sir."

Mac grins. "Ye never can be too careful, lass."

No. I suppose not.

I'm not sure how long Connor has been an enforcer for Hawk and the FCO but his maturity and experience shine through. I can only hope that once Lukas, Dune, Tundra, and I begin working together more often we can reach the same level of efficiency.

"How many enforcers do you command, Mac?"

"Och, weel, that depends on what the assignment is and how dangerous. As a rule, Mr. Barron generally sends out two to four squadrons at a time. Usually, each will have a squadron leader, but I tend to have seniority. Why do ye ask, lass?"

"I don't know how familiar you are with our situation here, but a bitch queen usurper slaughtered our entire royal army and the generals who commanded it. I've inherited the honor of rebuilding but other than Lukas, who I believe you know, no one else on my team has the experience to lead warriors."

"Och, I know Lukas well enough to say yer in good hands. If

he's committed to getting yer warriors where ye need to be, ye'll have no problems."

I laugh. "Except for the fact that I have no warriors to train. We're starting from scratch. I think that's why it's been such a pleasure working with you. Your men are well trained, they take direction well, and they get the job done without complaint."

Connor Mac casts a warm glance across the grounds, taking in the efforts of his teams. "Aye, weel, yer right about that. Hawk Barron, and by extension, Lukas, demand greatness from their enforcers. The men and women who serve the FCO rarely disappoint."

My wrist buzzes with the notification of an incoming text. I turn my arm to read the message on the screen.

Hey, babe. All is well. Tracking Brant and Hawk now. Dune arrived in time to save our butts. Thanks for sending him. Love you big.

I can't help the smile that breaks on my face as I read Lukas's words. My mates are all well. Shadow is safe in the castle and the others are safe and together.

There's a great deal of comfort in that.

My mind shifts to the fifth and newest member to the mating and I take the moment to message him and find out how things are going inside the King's Tower.

Shadow's response takes a moment, but in his defense, I'm sure it's hard to get a wolf cub to stare at his watch long enough to text me. Maybe Rhylan can adapt his watch to accept dictation and voice commands.

I make a mental note to ask the dragon about that.

After a brief moment, my wrist buzzes with Shadow's response. *Not well, I'm afraid. There's an issue with Calli's delivery. The medical devices Doc needs are unavailable to him because of the lockdown. No one is saying much, but there is a great deal of tension. Apologies, lirimaer, I wish I had better news.*

The floor drops from under me, and I realize it's been hours since I last checked in on Calli and how she was doing. Calli has always been indestructible, unstoppable... and now she's a freaking phoenix.

"Is everything all right, lass?"

"No. My bestie is in labor inside the castle, and the lockdown has complicated things. I need to go see if I can help."

"Of course. Do what you need to do. Should we proceed with clearin' out yer home in the forest or should we wait for ye to be available?"

I scratch my head my mind spinning.

Hawk has enough confidence in his team to let them handle situations. I do too. "No, you and your men go ahead. It's a straightforward objective. If there are men in Amberloq Hall, there shouldn't be. Get them out."

"And where would this building be?"

I point to the bronze roof glistening in the sunlight above the canopy of the forest. "You see that building there? That's Amberloq Hall."

Mac follows my pointed finger. "Consider it done."

Dune

Lukas, Tundra, and I leave the clearing full of angry goblins and navigate the afternoon sky. The heat from the midday sun is oppressively hot on my wings and back. The only thing making it bearable is that flying creates a breeze that cools things down.

Joining the day's plan already in motion, I'm not sure where we are headed or how long it will take us to get there. For the moment, I'm simply enjoying the quiet companionship of being airborne with Tundra.

And when I use the word 'quiet', I don't mean it in a literal sense because nothing about this flight is quiet.

I glare over at the four metal blades cutting through the air. I understand the appeal for land-bound humans to be able to conquer the skies, but could they do it by making a quieter vehicle?

At least then, maybe the rest of us could have a conversation. Just saying... or *not* saying because, hell, no one would hear me anyway.

I gauge by the rumble in my stomach we've been flying for a few hours when Lukas starts to descend.

The time for interaction is quickly coming to a head.

And while things went well with Tundra before we took off, it's never as easy with Lukas. That guy gets on my nerves. I realize a lot of that is my insecurity but hey, I never said I was perfect.

Well, yeah, I'm sure I have... but I realize I'm not.

We continue a gentle descent and I scan the surroundings below. The place where I caught up with them a few hours ago was in the remote landscape near the edge of the Dornte Fringe.

Now we are deep in the Badlands.

I've heard stories all my life about the kind of lawless bedlam one finds in the Badlands and I'm both excited and anxious about whether this place will live up to its reputation.

Unlike the Fringe, the Badlands seems to have a great deal of activity in the towns we flew over. And as unaccustomed and uninterested as they might be to seeing strangers, they came out in droves to stare up at the sky and gawk at the monstrosity Lukas is piloting.

How something so sleek and streamlined can disturb the peace so thoroughly seems like poor design to me. The feathers of the Elbirfae allow us to fly in silence. It's stealthy and gives us the advantage.

In this instance, we need to land a fair distance from where we need to be or there will be no stealth in our arrival. Considering lives depend on us getting behind enemy lines and finding missing warriors, I question whether Lukas's presence is a help or hindrance.

He lands the helicopter fifteen minutes after passing the last town and I suppose that's far enough so that not everybody below will know we're coming.

Of course, I can't voice my opinion of disapproval because despite my being right about the strategic loss of surprise, no one likes to hear my thoughts when it comes to our mating golden boy—Lukas the Precious.

When he sets down the bird and cuts the engines, I exhale a heavy breath. "Wow, that silence is a relief."

Tundra casts me a sidelong glance. "Careful what you say, Dune. The helicopter offered us a great advantage last night. We brought an entire squadron of warriors with us when we went to check out an enemy base camp. There are not enough Elbirfae Amberloq left for us to be purest snobs."

I chuckle. "No one has ever accused me of being a purest snob. If anything, I'm the one being pointed at for not complying with societal expectation."

Tundra grins. "That's very true. So, you know how it feels. Be thoughtful of our new reality and resist your first instinct to make a snarky comment."

I hold my hands up in surrender. "Before you start rhyming off all my faults, how about a Hey, Dune, glad you're here."

Tundra stretches his neck and exhales. "I'm sorry. Old habits. Hey, Dune. I'm glad you're here. We were all terribly worried about you the past two days. I'm relieved you're alive and well. Thank you for joining us and saving my butt back there."

Before I have a chance to say anything back, Tundra steps in and kisses me. And it's a great kiss too. Over the years, the two of us have gotten together out of frustration, desperation, and boredom, but this feels different.

Tundra's thumb brushes over my cheek as his lips gently but assertively relay his welcome. When he eases back, his mouth quirks up in a crooked smile. "I'm sorry, I should've done that sooner. I'm glad you're here."

I touch my lips.

Admittedly, the gentle affection routine is a new one for us and I'm a little thrown. "I, uh... that was nice. Thanks. I've had a couple of really shitty days and that was nice."

"You're welcome."

I scratch my head and am still a little dazed by that kiss when Lukas steps out of the helicopter and makes his way over to join us. "Dune, it's good to see you. Your arrival to join the fight was great timing."

"Yeah, I bet Tundra was even happier to see me considering he was getting his ass kicked and you were doing nothing to help him."

Tundra curses and rolls his eyes. "Is this you resisting your instinct to be snarky?"

I shrug. "What can I say? I'm a work in progress."

Lukas waves off Tundra's defense. "He's not wrong. When I saw you getting overwhelmed, everything in me wanted to jump out of the helicopter and join the brawl but you were right to wave me off. It was important to get the helicopter and get the hell out of there. Once I saw Dune flying in on the horizon, I knew you'd be all right. Believe it or not, I have faith in him."

I'm not sure I believe that, but I won't argue.

As Tundra said, this is our new reality and if I'm going to make it work, I've got to put in the effort. "So, fill me in. Where are we and why are we here?"

"Last night," Tundra says, "I took a call at the security office at Thornebane Castle. The woman I spoke with described weapons being fired at a barn not far from her home. Based on the description of the noise made by the guns, we presumed they were weapons from the other realm."

Lukas finishes locking up the helicopter and adjusts the straps of a supply backpack. "We organized a mission party for an intel-gathering trip to check out the lead. When we got there, everything pointed to the weapons being from the human realm, so we moved in."

I can tell by the frown on Tundra's face it didn't go well. Well, that and Honor telling me the team got ambushed last night.

"Not long after the ground teams moved in and infiltrated the barn, a bomb went off and most of the FCO officers were caught inside. I was able to go in and find Lukas, but he was hurt badly, and I needed to evacuate him to tend to his injuries."

"And while you did that, you lost track of the other men?" I ask.

Lukas nods. "Yeah, that's about it. This morning, we started tracking Brant and Hawk using the GPS locators on their tactical watches. And here we are."

I glance around, taking in the desolation of the scenery, and the remoteness of the area. Unlike where I found them in the Fringe, this place at least has treed areas and rock elevations. Although the Badlands are known to be less hospitable than the Fringe, the landscape doesn't seem to know that.

"So where are they from here?" I ask.

Lukas points over my right shoulder and I twist to follow the trajectory. There's a small clearing and then a heavily wooded area in the distance. "Two miles that way, according to the GPS coordinates."

I check the height and location of the sun to get my bearings and scan the tree line for any movement or sign that we might be walking into a second ambush. "So, are we hiking in or flying in with one of us carrying you?"

A glance passes between Tundra and Lukas and the two of them share a private smile.

It's Lukas who breaks the silence though. "I need to piss like crazy, and I wouldn't mind getting something into my stomach before we take on the next battle."

Tundra turns towards the trees like a fire has been lit beneath him. "I can find you some edible barks and berries if you're hungry."

Lukas chuckles and unzips the breast pocket of his flak vest. Sliding his fingers into the opening, he comes out with several green cellophane wrappers and grins. "I'd rather eat raspberry protein bars but if you want to eat bark, don't let me stop you."

Tundra extends his hand. "No, your menu selection sounds much better. You win."

Lukas rips open the wrapper and offers us each one of the bars sealed inside.

I haven't eaten anything all day and accept with genuine thanks. "When we regain control of Amberloq Hall, I'm going to stock the oculus room with non-perishables."

I accept another bar and try not to devour it like I'm an animal, but I'm slecking hungry.

When the three of us have hastily shoved a few protein bars in our mouths and are chewing, it becomes obvious I'm not the only one who's ravenous.

"How many of those bars do you have?" I ask.

Lukas finishes chewing and swallows. "Clearly, not enough. When we get back to the castle, I'll arrange for us to have the biggest, juiciest steaks sent to Amberloq Hall so we can grill them up and fill our bellies. We'll have baked potatoes and vegetables and a couple of cases of beer to wash it down."

My stomach growls at the suggestion and I pat my hand against the rumble. "You talk a good game, magic man. I look forward to you coming through on that promise."

"Until then, this is all I've got." He pulls another package out of his pocket and we go the route of protein bars once more. "And now that we're fueled up, let's roll out and find our men."

The three of us strike off towards the forest and now that

I'm thinking about it, I need to piss too. Hunger and a full bladder aren't much of a shared interest, but I guess having anything in common is better than nothing.

Baby steps, I suppose.

~

Shadow

Moonshade and I keep to ourselves for most of the morning, trying to stay out of the way as Doc, Jaxx, Kotah, and Keyla remain on baby delivery duty. The four of them have worked tirelessly through the night to keep Calli comfortable, her spirits up, and her labor going smoothly.

Well, as smoothly as it can go with no monitoring equipment, nothing to help her with the pain, and no idea what it takes to birth a phoenix young.

Thankfully, whatever Doc was originally afraid of hasn't manifested as an obstacle...

Or at least not yet.

That's not to say things are going well because I don't believe they are. Calli's water broke almost sixteen hours ago, and she's been laboring for more than twelve.

"Any improvement?" I ask Creed when he returns from checking on Keyla and the situation. Creed is staying out of the way too, although he spends the majority of the time either upstairs or in his study working.

"Regarding the baby... no. Regarding our state of being under siege... I hope so. Since the raid was downgraded, and everything is under control, Rhy and Honor should soon reestablish communication within the castle. Once that's done, hopefully, we can back out of this lockdown a few hours early and get Calli help."

"Reestablish communication?"

"Yes. Soon after the raid began, all communication channels in the castle went down. I'm assuming the goblins jammed things somehow."

I scrub my fingers over the ache growing in my forehead and ignore the dull ache gaining power. "My apologies. I didn't realize you need to communicate outside the King's Tower. I've been texting Honor using my tactical watch. If you have something you want to say to her or Rhylan, I'm happy to give you access to it."

Creed looks at me, and I can't tell if he's angry or frustrated. "I didn't realize you've been in contact with people outside these walls. Yes, of course, I need to speak to Rhylan and my sister. Calli's in trouble. We need to do something to get her the help she needs."

A loud banging sounds at the double doors of the grand entrance. Someone is pounding on the doors to the royal suite and giving them a beating.

"Creed? It's me. Shadow says Calli's not doing well. How can I help?"

The king rushes out to the entrance and places his palms against the inside panel of the door. "We need the lockdown lifted. Rhylan and I put it on a twenty-four-hour timer but I need him to find a way to end it sooner. Calli needs to be in the clinic downstairs and Doc could really use the help of some equipment and med-techs."

"All right, I'll contact him and see what I can do."

Moonshade has her nose pushed against the crease between the two doors while her tail wags wildly.

"Do you smell Honor, sweet girl?"

Moonshade sits on her haunches lifts her chin and lets off the eerie howl of a young wolf.

"I hear you, baby girl," Honor says from the other side. "I wish I was in there with you for a snuggle. As soon as we get this lockdown taken care of, we'll get Calli sorted out, take a long walk through the forest, reclaim Amberloq Hall, and snuggle for days."

"That sounds like heaven, *lirimaer*," I say. "Was the offer only open for the cute and cuddly spirit wolf or the rest of us too?"

"Oh, it'll be a no man is left behind event."

I chuckle. "Excellent, then let's get these doors open and Calli down to the clinic. She's been asking where Brant and Hawk are all night. I assume they are just as anxious to be in here as we are to be out there."

The silence that follows makes the hair on the back of my neck stand on end. My watch buzzes against my wrist and I crouch down and hold my arm out for Moonshade to look at.

"She's asking who is on our other side of the door?" I whisper.

"Just Shadow and me," Creed says. "Why? What's going on that you don't want someone else to hear?"

Honor spends the next few minutes explaining about the ambush and how Brant and Hawk are currently missing. "Lukas, Tundra, and Dune have gone on a search and rescue mission, and from what Lukas says, he's confident they are alive, and we can get them back."

"Oh, they're alive," Creed says. "The Phoenix Quint is bound and even if Calli is in too much turmoil to sense a disruption like Hawk and Brant being hurt or killed, Jaxx and Kotah would certainly feel it."

"Good point," Honor says. "I hadn't thought about that, but yeah, that's encouraging. I'll let you know as soon as I hear any updates from them."

Creed chuffs. "We certainly won't bring it up. Everyone is stressed enough in here as it is."

I straighten and press my palm against the door, wishing I could hold Honor in my arms. "You sound tired, sweeting. Are you well?"

"Well enough for now. I'm running on empty and am

balancing a dozen things at once, but things have gone well. We are definitely the victors of this battle."

Creed lets off a long sigh and I hear how the night has taken its toll on him. "That's excellent news. I'm proud of you, Honor. Now, our priority is to get this lockdown lifted so we can get Calli the help she needs."

"Agreed. Leave that with me. I'm on it."

CHAPTER SIX

Lukas

*T*undra, Dune, and I make short work of hiking the distance between where I landed the helicopter and where the GPS coordinates show Hawk and Brant are being held. My first trip into the Badlands is eye-opening.

It feels like I'm a character living in a Mad Max movie or maybe an episode of the Walking Dead.

Discarded vehicles lay rusted-out and left to play the part of planters for wild things to grow through. The forest is dotted with remnants of old campsites abandoned in a hurry by some long-forgotten survivor. And in the trees, we find some truly bizarre things… like a refrigerator or a shed door, and no explanation as to how it got up there or what purpose it served.

"This place is messed up," Dune says. "It's like a drug-induced nightmare brought to reality."

I agree.

Tundra brings his wrist up to check our bearings and taps the screen of his watch. "If I'm understanding this properly, the two of them should be in the next valley."

To call what we've been going through a valley is generous. It would be more accurate to say the landscape here has repetitive dips and rises which create the effect of sunken bowls into the earth.

Regardless, we all know what he means.

I raise my hand and signal for us to go quiet. Pointing to Dune I signal for him to take the left flank, Tundra to take the right, and that I'll continue forward on the path. As with each of these small valleys, there is a gradual rise in the pitch that crests gently before dropping into a concave gorge.

This time is no different.

I crouch as I climb the crest and drop to my hands and knees to peer over the ridge and assess the holding area before us.

What the fuckety-fuck?

When Dune said this place was messed up, he didn't know half of it. Now that we're looking down at what can only be considered a fae concentration camp we have to reassess the entire rescue plan.

The gorge below is entirely sealed off by a metal grid spread across the top of the valley like a lid on a pot. And by the hum of power and the hair rising on my body, the entire grating system is electrified.

With our forward progress blocked, both Dune and Tundra crawl back along the ridge to lay next to me to assess the situation and determine our next move.

"What's going on down there?" Tundra asks.

I shift to the side shrugging out of my backpack so I can unzip the side pocket. Pulling out my binoculars, I lay flat on my belly, adjust the scope settings to focus the vision, and take in the sights. "Holy fuck."

"What?" Dune asks. "What do you see?"

I hand the binoculars to him so he can see for himself. "Is this real? Am I seeing what I think I am?"

Tundra reaches across in front of me, eager to have a look

for himself. It doesn't seem like Dune wants to share but he relinquishes hold on the binoculars and lets Tundra have a turn.

He presses the eyepieces to his face and lets off a gasp. "By the Powers—Elbirfae. Hundreds of them."

Dune jumps to his feet and staggers back from the edge. "We are not extinct. Our families are down there waiting to be rescued. We're not the only two."

Tundra gets up to join him in an ecstatic hug.

The two lock tight and there's back-slapping and wing-flapping and more than a few happy tears.

It's a nice moment.

It's also heartwarming to see the emotion on Dune's face. With the torment of finding their homes empty and destroyed weighing on them, I was gearing up for him being more difficult than ever.

This is a pleasant surprise.

I set the binoculars on the ground and get up to join them in a celebratory hug. "I'm so incredibly happy for you." I hug Tundra and then Dune.

It's the first moment we've shared genuine physical affection and I admit, it's better to have his arms around me in an embrace than it was in a tackle where he's trying to kill me. "Congratulations to you both. I know how deeply the loss of family and friends resonated with you. It's wonderful we have a chance to end that suffering."

"Oh, we're ending it." Dune steps back and rushes to lay on the ground by the ridge again to get another look. "We're getting them out of there right now."

Tundra and I join him on the ground and I take another look at the electrified grid. "The question is, how do we rescue them?"

"Now that we are this close, do you think we could communicate with Hawk and Brant?" Dune asks.

I brush the dirt off my palms and consider that. "No. I don't think so. If they were still wearing their watches, they would've contacted us. Because they didn't, I assume either the belongings of prisoners are confiscated or maybe there's a jamming device."

"The raiders at the castle used one. It makes sense that they would block all frequency here. They wouldn't want any of the prisoners to call for help."

"But it can't be a complete block of signal," Tundra says, "otherwise we wouldn't have been able to track the GPS signal."

I accept the binoculars back from Tundra and take another look. "You're right about that, T. I bet they took the watches not knowing what they are and dropped them in a pile somewhere with everyone else's stuff. If you are right about the goblins not being the brightest bunch, they likely don't even realize what they are."

Dune frowns. "It couldn't have been the goblins who set this camp up. The Elbirfae were kidnapped and killed by Laryssa and the Blood Witch during the early days of the raids. If they put this camp together, the queen certainly would've considered tracking devices and spelled against them."

"Agreed. I came up against them more than once. They were both smart and incredibly powerful. Their downfall was arrogance. If the witch spelled this area to block detection, she may not have put anything in place in the event she was killed."

Tundra looks at me and arches an ebony brow. "You started a chain of events when you brought her down. First freeing Honor from her grasp and now this."

"You don't know what you don't know," I say. "The important thing is we know they're here now and we get them out of here as soon as possible."

"We'll need reinforcements," Dune says. "There's no telling how many guards they have down there for that many hostages."

I nod and flip my wrist over to call for backup. "Then it's a lucky break we have a few hundred FCO enforcers in the quadrant who can help."

Dune smiles. "And when you say help, you mean help us kick their asses, right?"

I chuckle and finish with my all-call request. "Oh yeah, we're going to obliterate these assholes."

"Finally, something you and I agree on. See, miracles do happen."

I nod, pleased Dune and I have finally found some common ground. "It's a good start."

~

Honor

It takes us an hour, but Rhylan and I finally get the lockdown sequence reversed. The metallic hum of the protective screens rising is music to my ears. "I have a med-tech team waiting outside the doors to the King's Tower," I say to Creed. "They will transport her to the clinic and have access to all the equipment needed for a difficult delivery."

Creed's breathing is elevated on the other end of the call. "Okay, I'm at the doors now... Yep, they are unlocked... and the med-tech team is here."

I clutch my fingers and meet Rhylan for a celebration fist bump. "I'm on my way. Get Calli the help she needs to deliver my niece and tell her I love her."

"Will do. And great job to you both."

The call ends and I flop into the closest chair to take a load off. I haven't sat for hours, I haven't slept for days, and I haven't had a chance for any of it to sink in.

"I'm taking a twenty-minute personal break to visit my mates and regroup. You want to come with me?"

I extend my hand into the air in front of me and Rhylan pulls me to my feet. "These are the moments I wish I was born with the power to teleport."

"I know that feeling. Some days the distance from this office to the King's Tower feels like it's a million miles away."

"Like now," I say, forcing my feet to move.

"Yeah. Definitely like now."

The two of us trudge our way out of the security area, through the castle proper, and make our way to the King's Tower. It's heartening as we pass through the castle public areas, the fear and panic of last night seem to have dissipated.

There is still a sense of upheaval, but we weathered the raid well and the citizens recognize that.

I'll take the win.

When the two of us arrive at the royal quarters, the guard at my brother's door clenches his fist and presses it to his chest in tribute.

"Congratulations, to you both," he says. "It's a pleasure to serve."

"Thanks, Sacaton," Rhylan says. "Were you here alone all this time?"

The guard shakes his head. "Our shift relief is on the way, so I sent Andros to his quarters to be with his young bride. She was shaken by the night's events, especially knowing her husband was standing between goblin raiders and the king."

Rhylan nods. "That's perfectly understandable. I'm home now and won't leave until the new guard shift arrives. Go eat and get some much-needed rest. Thank you for standing between the goblin raiders and my family."

"Thank you, sir. Always a pleasure, Princess."

When we step inside the suite, Rhylan locks the doors and then we're met by our welcoming committee.

Creed meets Rhylan chest-to-chest and closes his eyes to soak in the embrace before moving to me. My brother's hug infuses me with some much-needed energy and I'm thankful for the recharge. "You both did so well. Thank you for being on the front lines. If I had any say in it, I would've been out there with you."

I chuckle and step back. "And what good would that do us if the king isn't secured?"

"Well, Creed the King understands he needs to be secured but Creed the man, mate, and brother wish he was out there with you."

I chuckle. "Fair enough."

"So, it's over?" Creed asks.

"If you don't mind, I'll let Rhylan catch you up on everything that happened and how we handled it. I want to see Calli and hug Shadow and our little wolf."

Creed nods. "Go see Calli. You'll have to wait a moment for Shadow and Moonshade. The two of them took the first opportunity to go into the forest. The little pup did her best to adapt to confinement, but we could all tell she needed to be outside."

"Then I'm happy the two of them are getting some fresh air. I'll check in with my bestie and find him when I'm done."

Despite Shadow telling me things had been rough for Calli through the night, finding Keyla and Doc hugging in the hall outside her bedroom door brings the reality slamming home. The two of them look exhausted and emotionally wiped out.

"I'm sorry to interrupt. Can I go in?"

They ease apart and Keyla wipes her tears with her palms. "The med-tech gave her something to ease discomfort and she fell asleep immediately. If you don't mind, can your visit wait until they get her settled downstairs in the clinic?"

I wave her concern away. "If she's finally resting, I won't disturb her. That's much more important."

My wrist vibrates with an incoming notification, and I glance down to read it.

"Is something wrong?" Keyla moves closer and places a gentle hand on my elbow. The subtle spread of calm and strength is more welcome than she knows. "Your emotions went erratic there for a moment."

"Lukas is checking in. They followed a lead from the raid at a barn and discovered a concentration camp. They're guessing close to three hundred Elbirfae and other citizens are confined in a valley in the Badlands. He's asking that the FCO enforcers be sent to his coordinates for a rescue."

"That's wonderful news," Keyla says.

"It is, no question. My concern is rooted in taking away from castle security. What if I drain the resources of the FCO enforcers here and there is another wave of violence?"

"You have to send help," Doc says.

"I know." I run my fingers through my hair and fight the urge to drop to the ground in a puddle of exhaustion. "I'll go speak with Creed and Rhylan. We'll come up with a plan to handle this. Please tell Calli I was here and give her my love when she wakes up."

Keyla squeezes my arm. "Of course. Good luck."

I retrace my steps and return to the front entrance. Creed and Rhylan have moved into the great room to talk and as I arrive at the entrance, the front door opens and Shadow and Moonshade come bounding inside.

"Sweeting, you're here."

I cover my mouth as a yawn escapes and feel the flush of embarrassment warm my cheeks. "Sorry, that wasn't at all indicative of how I feel about your arrival."

Shadow chuckles and strides straight towards me. When he stops in front of me, he holds out his hands and I realize Moonshade is sniffing my boots.

He can't see me.

Stepping forward, I complete his approach and hug him, resting my head on his shoulder. "You don't mind if I stay here forever, do you?"

"Not one bit. Consider your invitation open-ended."

I close my eyes for a moment and breathe him in. His foray out into the woods with his baby wolf has left his skin smelling like fresh air and evergreens.

Sadly, I have to give it up for now. "As much as I'd love to stay, I just got the text from Lukas and need to talk business with Rhylan and Creed for a moment."

"Would you like me to leave?" Shadow asks.

I take his arm and lead him toward the couches. "Of course not. You're as much a part of all this as any of us. Come sit with me while I fill everyone in."

Once we're seated, I scroll back through Lukas's message and read it to the three of them. When I finish, Creed steps back looking stunned. "Wow, rescuing three hundred people is a massive undertaking."

"I know. Hawk's enforcers are amazing but I also don't want to be overconfident in our victory here and take our strongest defense team into the Badlands."

Rhylan sighs. "Those are valid concerns, but I think the reward far outweighs the risk. If we can rescue three hundred citizens from confinement and prove those people were taken by Laryssa and then held by Ruic Breard, we'll gain incredible support from the masses."

Creed nods. "Rhy's right. At the moment, some citizens favor Breard's rhetoric simply because they consider the Thornebane's weak after the raids. If we can prove that not only are we strong enough to defend the castle but at the same time rescue a large number of hostages, those opinions should sway to our advantage."

"But politics aside, are we in a position for me to take the FCO enforcers away from the castle?"

Creed looks to Rhylan for his opinion and they seem just as uncertain as I am.

"There is no option," Creed says. "You have to go and take as many warriors as you think we can spare."

"We'll talk to Mac," Rhylan says. "He's been instrumental in coordinating the FCO forces since they arrived. He has more experience in things like this than we do, and he might have the answers we need."

I like the sound of that logic. "Great idea. I sent him to assess the status of Amberloq Hall. I'll go find him and get things figured out and underway."

"Do you want me to come with you?" Creed asks.

"No, you two enjoy a few moments without chaos. I'll text you with the plan before I leave and give you a chance to have a say."

"Excellent," Rhylan says. "I wasn't sure how I was going to get off this couch."

"So stay and relax. I'll find Mac and let you know."

"And we will accompany you," Shadow says. "Won't we Moonshade?"

Our little ebony wolf cub bounces around our feet before checking in with us and racing towards the door. I link my arm with Shadow's and chuckle as we walk shoulder to shoulder toward the exit. "It's a wonder you don't get motion sick the way she tears around here like a hurricane."

Shadow squeezes my hand against his arm. "Oh, I definitely do. I've been close to vomiting for the past two days but I am so grateful to have her in my life I try not to let it bother me."

I lean my head to rest against his shoulder. "You're a very special man, Shadow. I'm grateful to have you both in my life."

CHAPTER SEVEN

Tundra

*D*une and I spend the next hour making our way around the circumference of what we've begun calling Hostage Valley. Looking at it from all angles, it's more like a sunken compound but however you view it, there are a lot of innocent citizens trapped down there. And now it's our job to get them out.

Lukas instructed us to pay special attention to the access points where the gatekeepers can release the metal grid to allow entry. As well, we're gathering the intel of how many buildings, guards, and outposts are inside fortifying their control.

By the time we make our way back to Lukas, we have a solid understanding of what we're facing as we plan for infiltration.

"What did you boys find out?" Lukas lifts his pencil from where he's jotting down notes onto a small pad. "How do they get the prisoners inside? Since there are four-wheelers and dirt bikes down there, I'm assuming there's a gate somewhere."

I lift my watch and access the compass. "There is an outpost due east," I extend my arm across the circle in front of us as if it's the face of a clock. "There are also two long, barrack buildings built along the rim over there. They back against the side of the steep slope of the valley wall."

"So, the grid is one solid, uninterrupted metal grate and they get inside by digging under it."

"That's how it appears, yes."

Lukas goes back to his notes and makes some adjustments. "That helps a lot. My concern was if we tried to cut through the metal or interrupt the power keeping the grid charged, we could set off alarms. If the entire metal grid is an uninterrupted disk, they've simply dug down to get beneath it, in theory, we can do the same."

"Unless they extended the structure of the grid into the ground," Dune says.

"True, there is that, but I have a feeling Laryssa and the Blood Witch were shortsighted on this being a long-term containment facility. They certainly didn't expect to both be dead within two years."

"Thankfully they are," I say. "I'm not sorry to say I'm glad."

Lukas shakes his head and gestures toward the valley. "No one in their right mind could see this place and argue against you. Those bitches had to go."

"Now we're left with the mess they made." Dune takes the binoculars and lays on his belly so he can prop up on his elbows and scan the grounds below.

"How serendipitous is it that the rebels are using it as their prison?" Lukas's excitement creeps into his voice. "Hawk and Brant's capture led us straight to this place. If it hadn't, we might never have found it and your people might never have had a chance to be free."

"That *is* amazing," Dune says without looking back at us. "But it's frustrating and degrading to be locked away for two

years and believe everyone has forgotten about you. I doubt the
people down there are celebrating that this is the prison of
choice."

Dune's pain pierces my heart.

I always prided myself as one of Valorous's trusted warriors.
When no one came back for us or even acknowledged we were
free to return to the Amberloq compound, it shredded our self-
worth.

And we felt that way and were safe and living in what people
would consider luxurious conditions. I can't imagine what these
people have gone through.

The sorrow in Dune's turquoise gaze is one of the most
honest emotions I've ever seen from him. "We have to get them
out of there."

"We definitely will." Lukas flips his notepad closed. "But
before we dig our way under this grating system to create an
access point, we have to decide where."

"What makes it a good spot to enter?" Dune asks.

I'm proud of him for asking the questions instead of
pretending he knows all the answers. This matters to him, I
know that. I'm sure he's feeling the same burgeoning hope as
I am.

We don't need to be the only two Elbirfae. There can be
others, there *are* others.

We just need to rescue them.

Lukas lays on the ground next to Dune and points into the
compound. "Do you see how the buildings are clustered along
the back half of the valley?"

"Yes."

"Well, whoever designed this camp, positioned things with
the understanding that everyone would be coming in the main
entrance. Behind those buildings, there is nothing but latrine
access and then the rising slope of the valley up to the grid."

"Right."

"So, unless you guys think otherwise, I say we dig our way under the grid there, so we have a straight shot down to the buildings."

"A straight shot down to the buildings also means the guards have a direct line of sight to us coming down that hill."

"During the day, absolutely, but by nightfall that visibility is gone."

"Unless the guards have night vision or night vision equipment," Dune counters.

"Exactly right. There's no way to get this done that has zero risk but if we choose the right access point and infiltrate during the window of time that gives us the greatest chance of success, we can do this."

I lay down beside the two of them and gesture for Dune to give me a turn with the binoculars. "So, what's our first step?"

"First, we choose three access points that can work to our favor. Then, we dig away the rim so we can get under this grid. And then, when the FCO backup teams arrive, we'll be ready to go."

Dune chuffs and makes a face. "And you think the three of us will have three access points dug and ready by the time the extra enforcers arrive? I saw you fly a helicopter here. I missed the part where you had backhoes and heavy digging equipment."

Lukas waggles his brows. "Work smarter, not harder. Who needs backhoes when we've got magic?"

Lukas

Tundra, Dune, and I make our way around the rim of the valley, staying back from the edge to ensure our presence remains undetected. Having given the two of them my thoughts on where we will set up our entry points, they point out what locations might work as we go.

I'm pleased to see the three of us can work together in a crunch.

I have no doubts about Tundra and me working together. He's an easy-going guy, respectful, and a pleasure to be around and work with. The same can't always be said for Dune but today is a new day and he's making a solid effort, so I do as well.

"If you agree on the other two spots, this is where I think the third access point would be best positioned." Tundra gestures to the land on our right where the electrified metal grid meets the rim of Hostage Valley.

"After looking at it from up here, I'm thinking maybe two points of entry might work better. The idea is to be able to slip down to the buildings below and given the distance between the buildings, I think three access points might be overkill."

"Is that what you truly think?" Dune asks, eyeing me up.

I shrug. "As opposed to what?"

"As opposed to you realizing you won't get the third access point dug before the FCO enforcers get here and you're trying to save face."

There he is.

There is the Dune I recognize.

"No. It has nothing to do with that. I honestly think three might be too much because I think we'd be sending men down on top of each other."

Dune doesn't argue. I'm not sure if he believes me or not but then again I don't care.

"So, unless one of you objects, I say we get to the digging. Like Dune said, I don't want to be caught making promises I can't keep."

Tundra rolls his eyes and is about to speak when I wave off his concern. "It's fine, T. No-fault, no-foul. I'm about to show you both why he's wrong."

With the flick of a hand, I gesture for them to step back and give me some room. Kneeling close to the edge of the lip, I press both palms against the cool earth and focus on creating a connection with the power of nature.

"Move Earth." I cast the spell and focus on the ground arcing along the rim. Obeying my command, the earth heaves and begins to shift creating a soil tidal wave pushing back from where the grid meets the ground.

To ensure no loose dirt carries down towards the compound below, I hold the connection longer than necessary but leave nothing to chance.

Easing back from the edge, I straighten, brush off my knees, and brush my palms together to rid them of dirt. "That's one done," I say, shooting Dune a shit-eating grin. "Let's head back to the spot where we chose for the first one."

Once I complete that access hole, the three of us step back and I check my watch. "Honor is arriving with the FCO backup in twenty. I'd volunteer to go meet them back at the helicopter, but one of the two of you would be much faster. Everyone has their skills, right Dune?"

I expect a smartass remark but instead, Dune dips his chin and smiles. "Point taken. That was badass and I stand corrected. Work smarter not harder."

The rumble of Tundra's deep laughter draws my attention. "I'll go meet the backup forces. Since the two of you are getting along so well, I don't want to break up the party."

I laugh at that, but the Iceman isn't wrong. The moments when Dune and I are getting along are few and far between. We need to build on those.

"Thanks, T. Safe travels. Bring them back as quickly as you can."

Tundra dips his chin, starts running towards the forest we came through, and launches off the ground. I expect him to arc up into the skies, but he stays low, navigating through the trees and remaining below the canopy.

It makes sense. With the number of Elbirfae being held captive, if one were seen flying anywhere near here, it would sound the alarms.

"So, Lukas," Dune says, suddenly growing tense and serious, "I've done a lot of thinking over the past few days, first when I thought my people had been slaughtered and then again last night when I was separated from everyone and locked down in the oculus room."

Oh, this should be interesting. "And what did you think about when your world was rocked, and you were left on your own?"

"I have issues to work through."

No shit. "Go on."

"I was the slecking bomb in my village and I grew up being treated like a king. I bought into the hype and when I became an Amberloq warrior it was a rude awakening to realize I wasn't that special. I overcompensated by being a dick."

"No argument. So, where do you go from here?"

He turns his face toward the sun and smiles as a breeze picks up his sandy, blond hair. "Honor punched me in the face the other day and told me I'm blowing it."

"We all told you as much, but good for her."

He chuckles as if he's remembering the assault with fondness. "Despite me screwing up, I've got lots to offer. I've been given the chance to be an Amberloq General, a mate to the princess of the quadrant, and a warrior in a battle I believe in. I have a dream life in the palm of my hand and I'm pissing it away. I don't want to do that."

"Well, I can honestly say I've noticed an improvement in your attitude today and it's been a nice change. I want us to be able to work with one another and not always be at odds. The mating stuff with Honor, Tundra, and Shadow progressed naturally. I'd like for—"

"Wait, what? Shadow? What does he have to do with our mating stuff?"

I run through the events of the past three days and realize he didn't know. "I'm sorry. You missed that. While you were gone the past few days, Honor and I invited Shadow into our mating foursome. We are now the Thornebane Quint."

He looks at me like I've grown a couple of extra heads and gone Hydra. "And Tundra and I don't get a say in it?"

I hold out my palms. "It's done. I'm sorry if it sideswiped you, but Tundra is cool with it and it was kind of you who set it all in motion."

"Me? How do you figure?"

"You instigated that damned Truth or Dare kiss."

Dune stills, frowning at me. "I knew there was more going on under the surface than a drunken collision of bodies. You two were way too hot for each other."

"Then you were the first to know and he and I had to catch up on what was obvious."

Dune steps away and sighs. "What does that mean for me?"

I scan the trees to ensure the two of us are still alone in our conversation. "What does what mean?"

"I mean… where do I fit in? You're gifted in the strategic part of things and a born take-charge guy. Tundra knows everything about the Amberloq and is the dependable one. Shadow is the sweet and understanding kind who listens and offers sage advice. Where does that leave me? I can't figure out how I fit into this mating and now it's even more complicated."

Dune's look of despair is so heartfelt, I ache for him.

I step forward and squeeze his shoulder. "You're you. That's all you need to be." He meets my gaze with a quizzical look, and I chuckle. "Preferably this more evolved, less dickish version of you."

That must be the right answer because his anxiety seems to ease, and he straightens. Standing this close together, I sense as the energy in the air shifts. There's no arguing that the guy is ripped and attractive. The cocky bravado even has its appeal.

Maybe it's not so ridiculous to think that we'll progress to being close. Well maybe.

Dune's gaze is searching my expression and by the flaring of his pupils and the ruffle of his feathers, he seems to be coming to the same conclusions. "I'll try. No promises, but I'll try."

⁓

Honor

Dusk is fast approaching by the time Tundra leads our group out of the trees. We parked the buses back near the helicopter to avoid being heard on our approach. If Hawk had a few more planes in the realm, we would've had other options but since there's only one, we portaled to the Fringe and then had to drive the rest of the way.

The only boon to the hours wasted getting here was the luxury of catching a few hours of sleep before the next war begins.

"There she is," Lukas says, striding over to pull me into his embrace. He smells like charcoal and manly musk and blood. "You look like hell, magic man."

"Thanks. Getting blown up tends to do that to a person. You should've seen me before I got back to the helicopter and changed."

"I'm glad I didn't. I don't want to think about you being mortal. In my mind, I prefer to envision all my guys as invincible."

"Noted." He brushes his lips over my forehead and spends an

extra moment kissing the bruise above my right eye. "How are you? Is everything all right at the castle? How's Calli?"

"I'm fine. I need a hot bath and to sleep for a few days straight, but I'll survive."

"I look forward to the bath. I'm invited, aren't I?"

"Always," I say, realizing too late that we're in the company of at least a dozen wildlings who can smell our growing affections for one another. Shutting that down, I get back to business. "The castle is good. Calli is struggling, but now that the lockdown is over and she has the medical support needed to have a baby, I'm hoping she and baby Liza will be fine."

He searches my gaze and I feel his reluctance to believe my account, but it's all I've got for him.

"I have to believe they'll be fine. The alternative is unacceptable."

"Like that, is it?"

I can't think about that right now. "When Tundra said he left you and Dune to spend time together, I was skeptical. I figured we'd arrive and find the two of you in the throes of killing one another."

Lukas casts a warm gaze over to Dune and beckons him closer. "Nah. We've been working on finding common ground. So far we both prefer fruit protein bars over Tundra's bark, we both want to rescue the people in Hostage Valley, and we both think you're the best thing that's ever happened to us and we don't deserve you."

I roll my eyes and blush. "Stop teasing me."

"No teasing, Princess," Dune says coming over to join us. "You're the real deal. We're going to make this quint something we can all be proud of. Wait and see."

I step out of Lukas's embrace and hug Dune. "I'm looking forward to it. Welcome home. We missed you."

When I step back, I gesture to the weird metal screen covering over a prison compound below. "All right. While you guys fill your bellies, let's run through what you know and get ready to rescue our citizens. Who's got the rations for my mates?"

"Here lass," Connor Mac says, raising a backpack and striding over to join us. "Eat up, lads. We don't want yer rumblin' bellies to give away our positions."

Lukas chuckles and accepts the bag. "Thanks, Mac. We'll try to keep it down. Now, gather round. It'll be dark soon and we want to move out as soon as possible."

CHAPTER EIGHT

Tundra

$\mathcal{W}$e spend the next twenty minutes going over the plan on how we're going to handle the infiltration and who's going where. The more I'm around the FCO enforcers in action, the more impressed I am.

They have a system of protocols for tactical events that I admire. As much as I admired Valorous during my years as an Amberloq warrior, she kept us sequestered and our training was more theory than practice.

These officers are accustomed to being in the thick of danger and it shows. They know what they are responsible for, and they need very little direction.

"What's on your mind, sweetie?" Honor asks me as I watch everyone assembling into their groups.

"No disrespect intended, but I was thinking Valorous did us a great disservice by elevating us to such an elite height. If our forces were accustomed to engaging with hostile fronts like these officers, we would've been better prepared to respond to Laryssa's attack."

"You think?"

"I do. The Amberloq warriors I served with were never as tactically prepared as these men and women. We had natural abilities, honed skills, and learned protocols but everything was based on theory. Your aunt left the policing to law enforcement and the castle security to the Royal Guard."

"I was thinking the same thing," Dune says, joining us. "These soldiers aren't great warriors because they performed training drills and understand protocols. They're great because they've spent time in skirmishes and tracking people down and battling the enemy."

Honor nods. "Great insights, guys. Let's come back around to that once everything is settled."

Before either of us has a chance to respond, Lukas signals for us to follow him. He steps away from the bustle of warriors getting amped up to access the valley and leads us into a small stand of trees a short distance away.

When we get to where we're going, he looks like he has something important to say.

"Is there a problem with the operation?" I ask.

"No. Not at all," Lukas says. "Beta squad left to establish a position at the entrance gate. Delta squad is moving to the first access point. We're with Alpha squad moving out from here."

"So, what's the look, magic man?" Honor asks.

"I just wanted a private moment with the three of you before the shit hits. I wanted a chance to tell you all to be careful and alert and if it comes down to the wire, to hang in there because none of us will ever stop fighting to get to you. We may not have it all figured out but this is happening and it's going to be amazing."

I put my arms out and take a step closer, corralling everyone to close ranks. "Agreed. Maybe it's the universe's will or fate or simply a random chain of events that brought us together, but together is where we are."

Dune steps forward and wraps one arm around my hip and one around Honor's. "Together is a good thing. I've spent years pretending I'm a one-man army and it's lonely. Together is where I want to be."

Honor leans to the side and kisses his cheek. "I know it hasn't been long enough for our footing to be rock solid but the feelings are real and the bonds are growing. I care about each of you and respect you as men, warriors, and friends. I'm proud to call you my mates."

Lukas looks from me to Dune to Honor. "The bonds *are* growing. The first chance we get, we lock ourselves in a room together and spend some time. Those bonds will flourish if we ever spend more than five minutes together. I'm looking forward to great meals and movie nights and drinking games."

"And sex," Dune adds. "If no one's going to address the obvious benefit to five in our mating, I will. There will be sex... lots of sex. I'm looking forward to that."

The seriousness of the moment is broken and we all get a chuckle out of that. Leave it to Dune.

Lukas grins. "Yes, and the sex. That will be amazing too, I'm sure."

"But until then, a good luck kiss is all we have the time and privacy for." Honor turns to me first and presses her hands against my weapons vest. "Be careful tonight, Tundra. I know you're determined to save your people but be safe."

"You as well, Princess." I take advantage of holding her in my arms and slide my lips along the smooth line of her jaw. She smells of summer blossoms and affection and I breathe her into the depths of my lungs.

Lifting my head, I claim her mouth for a kiss. She comes to me willingly and presses the warm rounds of her breasts against my chest. I flare my wings and fold them forward, wrapping her tight in my protective embrace. When I end the kiss, we're both breathless. "I wish there was more time and a mattress nearby."

Honor chuckles. "Me too."

We part and she moves to Dune.

I hug Lukas next, locking together in a moment of quiet before the storm. "Don't be the hero tonight, mate." I ease back from the hug and stand with our mouths inches apart. "I believe you owe me some naked time exploring this sexual tension we've been sharing."

Lukas chuckles. "Oh, yeah. I'm not going to risk that. I'll be careful and you do the same."

Our mouths meet and my mind fills with all the sensations we shared earlier this morning. The kiss is hot and aggressive and makes my heart flutter. I chuckle as we part and bite my lip. "That reminds me, I haven't submitted my comment card yet."

Lukas grins. "Right. We'll come back to that."

"Yes, we will."

I leave Lukas to spend a moment with Honor and I face Dune. He's come a long way in the past two weeks. I'm not surprised. I always recognized the potential he worked so hard to keep hidden.

Standing directly in front of one another, I set my hands on his hips. "Be mindful of your surroundings and remember there are people who value you and want you to come home safe after this is over."

Dune arches a brow. "Are you coming on to me, Iceman?"

"We're mated now. I don't think it's a come-on as much as me telling my mate I love him and care what happens to him."

Dune's eyes widen. "You love me?"

There's no going back now. "Goddess help me, but I do. I think I have for a long time but I didn't realize it because most of the time I could barely stand being in the same room with you without wanting to punch you in the face."

Dune laughs. "Oh, yeah. That's why I missed it."

The two of us meet with a force and familiarity that only

two people who have collided hundreds of times could share. The kiss is searing and filled with promises.

This is our new start.

When we step apart, he meets my gaze and grins. "It makes sense that you love me. I'm quite a catch."

I roll my eyes and step back, but he matches my movements and swallows. "I love you, too, Iceman. You are my lover, my mentor, and my friend. I think part of the reason we always fought so much is that we both knew it and didn't want to acknowledge it."

"Sounds about right."

He raises his arm and holds out a cupped hand. "I acknowledge it now. I'm proud to call you my mate."

I meet his grasp and pull him in for one last, brief kiss. "You should be proud. I'm quite a catch."

We're both chuckling as we part and the four of us look one another over. "So, this is us," Honor says.

"Four of the five, anyway," I say, making sure Lukas realizes we respect and accept our fifth member. "We'll have to catch Shadow up on what he missed when we get back to the castle."

"Yes, we will," Honor says. "But for now, it's time to get ready to rock and roll."

"I was born ready." Dune raises his hands and does a little dance. "Honestly, that's true. My nurse mother told me I came out with my fists up and my eyes open."

Lukas smiles. "I think we already established your nomadic family had an absurdly high opinion of you."

"I don't know if it was *absurdly* high."

A couple of days ago, that comment would've devolved into an argument. Today, the two of them laugh and head back to rejoin the others.

Mac turns from his men and smiles as we arrive. "All set?"

"All set," Honor says.

"How do you want to play this, Lukas?" Mac asks.

Lukas lifts his head and scans the crowd making sure everyone is listening. "Mac's got point with Alpha squad. Honor you're with me. Dune and Tundra, you've got our six. If you see anything coming at us, you have the best chance of swooping in to intercept because of your ability to fly."

"Consider your asses watched." Dune grins.

I give him a look. "Seriously? Get your head in the operation and stop acting like an ass."

"Oh, Frosty. Is the honeymoon over already?"

Honor and Lukas both chuckle and start moving toward our access point. Fine, if they're not bothered by his hijinks, I'll let things slide. After all, it's not my job to police him anymore.

He's my mate, not my trainee.

"Everyone test your comms," Lukas says, raising his finger to tap his earpiece. "Check. Check."

As he speaks, his voice resonates clearly in my ear and I nod. "Check."

When everyone is finished with the last checks, we position ourselves at the entrance of the hole Lukas dug and await the go.

"Alpha Squadron in position," Mac says.

"Beta Squadron in position," a woman says.

"Delta Squadron in position," a man says.

Lukas nods. "This is Team Leader. It's a go."

From that moment, everything goes silent. Mac's team leads the way down the slope and Lukas and Honor are tight on their heels. Dune and I are the sweepers, taking up the rear to ensure nothing unexpected comes from behind.

The slope of the valley is covered in short scrub. It's moist and thick enough to absorb the sounds of our progression but too low to conceal our presence.

As we descend, I tip my weapon and check the charge of my pulse cartridges. It's not at full strength but it's not far off.

Mac holds a fist in the air and the entire group stops and holds position. A guard has come around the building and if he looks up, he's likely to see nine people in black army gear a hundred yards above.

Too close to hide. Too far to silence him quickly.

I consider whether or not this is one of those 'swoop in' moments Lukas alluded to. As if he can read my mind, he turns back to me and shakes his head.

All right. So, we wait.

The guard doesn't seem to notice us at all and moves in to use the latrine. Once he's inside one of the wooden shacks, Mac turns to his men, makes a hand gesture toward the toilet and two soldiers break away.

The rest of us hold position while the dispatched soldiers close the distance to the latrine. One sneaks around to the front while the other remains at the back. The one at the back leans in close and is looking between the slats of the wooden wall.

When he lifts his weapon and presses it against the back wall of the latrine, the soldier at the front steps to the side. He's out of the line of fire but continues to hold the front door shut.

I don't know if they share a quiet signal or not but a moment later the soldier holding the door ducks back in front and returns with the body of a man killed with his pants around his ankles.

"A rather humiliating way to die," Dune whispers.

Lukas shrugs. "Looks good on him. Anyone involved in making this happen is a piece of shit."

Mac turns to us. "One less guard going forward."

We resume our descent and catch up to the other two soldiers who have pulled some loose wood and dried scrub over to cover the body hidden behind the latrine.

Once our group is back together, we finish our descent. The compound is a large circle with three sentry guards positioned in small, wooden towers. There are three main buildings and four outbuildings.

Lukas holds us back as Mac and his team disappear around the side of one of the main buildings. "We need to hit the sentries in a coordinated strike," he says. "We have snipers with each of the teams to get it done. It's our job to wait and be ready to move out."

"Tundra and I can take two of them out," Dune whispers. "We can fly up and end them. Not an issue. Can't we, T."

Lukas waves the idea off without consideration. "They're guarding Elbirfae. They're ready to defend against incoming hostiles. Our snipers will take them out from the shadows and they won't know what hit them."

Honor meets our gazes. "I have no doubt you could handle this, but these squads are a honed unit. Let them do what they do best. In the end, all we care about is rescuing the hostages. If Lukas's teams give us an edge, then we take it and learn from what they do."

"And what do we do?" Dune asks. "We're the Amberloq, aren't we?"

Lukas waves us in closer. "Of course, you are. Once the sentries are down, you two are our offensive line. I want you on the rooftops of the barrack buildings watching our backs while we move in to free the hostages. If there's trouble, you need to let us know."

"And what are your FCO soldiers going to be doing?" Dune asks.

"We counted nine guards. With the three in the towers and the one in the shitter, that leaves another five within the compound. The FCO men have been tasked to take out the enemy. We're on search and rescue."

Dune frowns but I see the wisdom. "We'll get our chance to shine. Tonight, our duty is to ensure the rescue goes off without incident."

"And you want Honor to take point on a front-line invasion? I'm not comfortable with that."

"Fuck you, Dune," Honor whispers. "I'm your commander. You don't decide what I can and can't handle."

"You're a walking target. You practically glow with radiance. There's no way these assholes are going to miss seeing you."

Lukas turns and frowns. "He's right. In the dark of night, your hair practically glows silver in the moonlight." He unzips a pocket on his vest and pulls out a black cap. "Put this on, babe. We don't want anyone targeting your pretty head."

She does as instructed but Dune still doesn't look happy. "I still don't like it."

Lukas gives him a sympathetic gaze. "I understand the need to protect her, but she's right. Even before she became the Guardian of the Crown, Honor was a proficient fighter. She's had hand-to-hand and weapons training her entire life. She may have been weakened by her confinement, but she's stronger every day and is as much of a force out here as we are."

Lukas passes an assessing gaze over our mate, and she winks at him. "Damn straight. I've been working every day on my physical conditioning. Don't put me in a princess box. I won't stay there."

The comm in my ear goes live and it's Mac's voice we hear next. "Four down. Wildlings are tracking the others. Position for rescue but hold for the go."

~

Honor

When Mac gives us the update and tells us to position for the rescue, Lukas and I make our way between the two buildings. Sticking to the shadows as much as possible, we arrive at the edge of the light that illuminates the courtyard of the compound. Mac told us to get into place and await our go order, so nothing to do but wait.

"Good luck, magic man," I whisper, leaning in for a kiss. Lukas's lips are warm and soft, and I wish I had more time—I don't.

"Be careful, babe. Stay tight to my ass."

"My favorite spot." I look up to the roofline of the two buildings beside us. I can't see Tundra and Dune, but I know they're there. The bond of our union is growing stronger and I feel them close by. "You too, boys. Keep it tight and be safe. I'm looking forward to getting home with all of you and having some quiet time."

"As are we," Tundra says.

"Yeah. Lots of mate things to revisit," Dune adds. "Looking forward to that."

I chuckle. I like this playful Dune. He's got the same smartass quips just without the edge of anger and entitlement laced through them.

Reaching up, I brush my lips across Lukas's and pause. He seals our mouths with one last, heated kiss, his tongue sweeping the seam of our lips to demand entrance. The show of affection holds all the passion and promises we share between us. This needs to work out.

We have a lifetime of magic ahead of us.

We part a little breathless but I'm not the only one whose chest is pumping.

This is what it's like with him.

We're swept away every time we're this close.

"Six sentries down," Mac says over the earpieces. "Beta squad has one sentry at the entrance. There is at least one unaccounted for."

Lukas meets my gaze and I nod in understanding. It's as good as it's getting. It's go time, regardless of there being opposition in the mix.

Stepping back, I give him the lead to check the coast is clear. I cast a last glance up at the darkness looming above the rooftops and send Tundra and Dune positive mental vibes. "Here we go, boys. Bad guys to end. Friends and families to rescue."

CHAPTER NINE

Lukas

I backflat against the edge of the building and check that our way is clear. The barracks buildings face an open area of well-trod dirt and grass and beyond that, service buildings look directly into the area we're about to enter.

There's movement in the shadows across the way, but those soldiers are with us...

I'm almost positive.

"All clear from up here," Dune says.

"Here too," Tundra adds.

"Roger." I draw a steadying breath, surprised I'm so apprehensive. This is a walk in the park for me but Honor being here changes everything. Hell, even Tundra and Dune being here makes this harder. "Still, I told them to trust Honor's skills. I have to do the same thing."

And with that, I launch forward and wrap around the front of the first building. Gripping the lock securing the door, I focus on a melt metal spell and reduce the shackle to a puddle on the ground.

It's painless, quick, and a moment later, I'm flipping the bracket of the padlock and easing the door open an inch to check for secondary deterrents.

"I've got a trip-line here," I say, cursing. "This is going to take a second."

"Is it wired to detonate, or can you cut it?" Mac asks.

"Yet to be determined." I flash my penlight into the sliver of an opening and crouch to follow the line.

"This is Delta-4. Another sentry down."

Good. The more opponents our teams find and take out, the better the chances that we're going to get out of here unscathed.

I follow the thin wire down to the bottom of the door and curse. "It's rigged to detonate and runs into a black box. I can't access it from this side of the door."

"Then either you need to wake up a helper or make a new door," Mac says.

"Agreed. Moving to the back of the building to make a new point of entry."

I turn and gesture for Honor to fall back. "Around the back. Plan B."

"What does that stand for, Plan bomb?"

I grin and the two of us hustle along the side of the building toward the back. "Plan don't explode the bomb and all the people inside."

"That's a good plan."

"I thought so."

Before we turn the corner to access the path at the back of the buildings, I check quickly that we've got no visitors to the latrines. When I verify all is well, I shrug off my backpack and pull out the thermal imaging camera. "Let's see what's happening inside, shall we?"

I power things up and wait for the orange and yellow heat sources to start appearing. There are a lot of bodies inside... most of them lying on the floor or low to the ground.

"Hold this and watch for any sudden shifts in position. Let me know if anyone's getting up or coming over. There might be hostiles planted within the group. We have to be ready for anything."

Honor takes the camera and holds it in place.

Reaching into my handy-dandy duffle, I grab the mini saw and cast a silencing spell to suppress the noise. Searching along the edge of the structure, I find the line of screws and position just above that.

The wood isn't much of an opponent against the four-inch diamond blade and soon enough, I've cut through six boards along the bottom and rise on my knees to go across again to make a three-foot square hole in the wall.

Plank by plank I remove the boards and set them on the ground before pointing to the next building. "I need to do the other building. Dune or Tundra, one of you come down off the roof and work with Honor on evacuating the hostages."

A moment later, Dune lands silently beside us and I point to the hole I made in the side of the building. "Take my penlight and be careful. Don't expect everyone in there to be happy to see you. They've been prisoners for over two years. We don't know what kind of conditioning they've endured."

Honor and Dune peer into the dark square I cut in the back of the building and begin their infiltration.

Once they crawl inside, I grab my tools and run in a crouch to repeat the process on the other building.

That's when everything goes to shit.

Tundra

When Lukas asks for one of us to drop down and help Honor with the rescue of hostages, Dune's reaction is immediate.

There's no conferring, no inquiry of which of us might go, no effort made to consider me at all. At first, I take it as him being as selfish as ever and then I catch sight of his face and realize it's more.

He's worried about Honor.

He's hurting that our races have been hurting.

He's so eager to protect the people he cares about that he's forgotten his considerations.

I decide to give him a pass and let him do what he needs to do. He's been trying today—genuinely trying.

Scanning the compound and the grounds beyond, I catch the figures moving in the shadows and watch to ensure they are friends and not foes.

Our men have taken the sentry towers.

The compound is secure.

Everything is going exactly according to—

"This is Beta-1," A woman says over the comm system. "We have an incoming convoy. Four military trucks tarped at the back. No way to know how many men. Please advise."

That's an easy call. They need to keep the reinforcements out of here and let us finish the rescue.

"This is Team Leader, stand down and hold position," Lukas responds. "Do not engage, Niah. Let them pass and we'll deal with them down here. We've got sixteen soldiers to your six."

"Roger, Team Leader. Holding position and standing down."

Right. For them to take a stand would pit the six soldiers of Beta Squadron against an unknown number of hostiles. Good call, Lukas.

"Alpha and Delta squads, take tactical ground and ready for company."

"Alpha Squad, roger."

"Delta Squad, roger."

"Dune and Honor, we've got incoming hostiles. Status report," Lukas asks.

Nothing comes back to us.

"Honor or Dune, what's your status?"

When the silence on the other end of the line stretches on, my pulse begins to race.

"This is Team Leader. Whoever is closest to the latrines call it out and get back here, ASAP. I need two men to evacuate the second building."

"Delta-3 responding."

"Alpha-4 responding."

"Tundra, you're with me."

He doesn't need to tell me twice. I run two steps and dive over the edge of the roof, tilting my wings to soar toward the ground and where Lukas is finishing the access hole in the second building.

I land beside him, and he straightens and draws his gun. When two soldiers arrive, Lukas points to the opening he made. "You boys free these hostages."

Then he gestures to me and tilts his head toward the other building. "Let's go find out why the fuck they're not reporting back."

Lukas moves quickly and I fall in line behind him.

It's only fifty feet between the two access openings but my anxiety is getting the best of me.

Lukas moves forward, with deliberate force. He's all military but carries magical energy that raises the hair on my arms. I've seen what he can do with his abilities.

He's incredibly powerful—far more powerful than his soldier persona implies. People seeing him might recognize him as a physical threat, but they'd be overlooking how lethal he can be.

Which only makes him more dangerous.

Lukas crawls through the opening and I follow. As soon as we're inside, a surge of power snaps in the air. The silence is broken the moment we're fully inside and we're blinking against the brilliance of all the lights being on. I straighten, searching our surroundings.

What *is* going on?

"Drop your weapons, boys, or Princess Thornebane is dead." I meet the piss-yellow eyes of the goblin grinning at us and then shift to where two forest Elbirfae are holding a dagger to Honor's throat.

"Release her, this instant," I snap, my wings flaring behind me. "She is your Amberloq General. How dare you take up arms against her."

"Easy, Tundra," Honor says. "It's not their fault. It's the collars they're wearing. They negate free will and force them to obey."

I scan the interior of the building. It's appalling to see more than a hundred Elbirfae fitted with the same silver choker across their throat.

Meeting the stunning green gaze of the brunette holding the dagger, I read the battle warring within her. "I'm sorry. This is not me."

"And this is how nine guards can keep hundreds of fae prisoner for two years," Lukas says.

"Trust us," a burly old desert male says. "If we could, we'd rip these slecking goblins in half."

Lukas grins. "Then, by all means, let's reinstate your choice and give you your chance."

With that, Lukas raises his palm and smiles. Magic snaps in the air, the pressure of it builds until it feels like a balloon about to burst. Then, when he snaps his fingers, the pressure breaks.

A wave of energy blasts through the room and the prisoners stagger to catch their balance. When they steady themselves, they shake their heads, and all the collars unlock and fall clanking to the wood floor.

The moment the new reality takes hold, the mood in the room shifts.

"Your free will is returned to you, and as much as I imagine you'd like to make this man suffer, four trucks are pulling into the courtyard and we need to go. A quick death is all we have time for."

"We're not going anywhere," the brunette says, releasing Honor. "Not until this place is destroyed and we're sure every prisoner here is free."

"I assure you they are free," Lukas says. "I disrupted all of the collars in this compound."

Her smile is both beautiful and determined. "You can stay or go, that's up to you, soldier, but we've been dreaming of this day for years. We will have our revenge against these slecking sacks of shit."

"Then I guess we've got a fight on our hands," Lukas says, tapping his earpiece. "This is Team Leader. What's our sitrep?"

When nothing comes back to us, Lukas frowns and looks around. "Let me guess. There's a signal jammer in here somewhere."

The brunette nods. "To ensure we're kept in a vault of helplessness, of course."

Lukas tilts his head. "I made you a back door to avoid the explosive charges. Anyone wanting to leave this place or unfit to battle, there are escape passages if you climb straight up the incline to the grid. Anyone wanting to fight, our teams are in all black. Don't kill my men and you're welcome to take up arms."

The brunette presses her shoulders back and nods to several of the other forest fae. "Glenn and Clover, you escort the elders and the injured out of this valley. Fox and Bay, seize the weapons from the north shed. Dusty and Clay, you're with me."

The woman is fierce and by the way everyone jumps into action, she has earned their respect. She doesn't wait for formal introductions, she directs her people out of the bunker at top speed.

"Well, alrighty then," Lukas says, waggling his ebony brows

and hustling to follow. "I don't know who she is, but she's got fire."

"That's Lark," a forest Elbirfae boy says. "She's in charge around here."

I'm about to comment on that when I'm knocked back and twist to see who is wrapped around my chest, hugging me. "Skye?"

The blonde tips her head back, her eyes filled with tears. The girl I knew in my village has grown up, the pure joy and happiness in her eyes has hardened.

"I knew you weren't dead." She seems to catch hold of her emotions and notices the attention. Pushing back, she punches me in the stomach and steps back. "You took your sweet time finding us."

My mind is still spinning when she joins the flow of exodus and leaves me wondering what went wrong.

"I see you were just as successful with women in your village as you were with the Amberloq," Dune says amusement thick in his voice.

"Skye is ten years my junior. There was nothing romantic between us. She lost her father in an avalanche and I sort of became her big brother. It seems life has been no kinder to her since I left my village."

"Today's a new day." Honor takes my hand, her amethyst eyes alive with warmth. "Once we get out of here, and settled, there will be plenty of time to make up for the chaos Laryssa caused."

"Agreed. The important part of that sentiment is once we get out of here. I suppose we should join the battle in progress."

Honor nods. "We will, but there are a lot of people here who are more invested in fighting for their justice. They need this for closure."

I understand what she's saying and agree. "Then we shall ensure the escape goes smoothly and provide backup support."

"A great idea." Honor scans the room to ensure everyone has gotten out and then the two of us join the back of the line to exit this prison.

Lukas

I leave Honor to oversee the evacuation of the prisoners in the barracks building. After crawling outside, I watch as a hundred or more Elbirfae climb the slope of the valley toward the holes I made to access this compound.

Everything seems to be going smoothly. Although, the gunfire in the compound at the front of the buildings is worrying. Drawing my gun, I race up between the two buildings to join the fight.

Joining the sea of bodies filing up toward the courtyard I continue my search. Hawk and Brant weren't in the first building but if the goddess is with us, they've been released from the second and are here somewhere.

"It's about time," Brant says, chuckling as I emerge from between the buildings. "We wondered if you'd ever get here."

"I told you," Hawk says, "now that he's mated, he's just not that into us."

I roll my eyes and flash them each a middle-fingered salute. "You're both assholes... and lazy too. What? You can't even join in to help with your own escape battle? Since when are you two wallflowers sitting on the sidelines? Are you getting old?"

Hawk chuckles and gestures towards the chaos in the courtyard. "Too many cooks in the kitchen. Mac and the squads are there to ensure the Elbirfae get their justice. We're just waiting for our ride back home to Calli."

"Yeah." Brant sobers. "Any news on our baby girl? Calli's going to kick our asses for missing the birth."

"Hey now," Hawk says. "Being blown up and kidnapped is a pretty good excuse."

There's no sense keeping anything from them. Might as well hit this head-on. "From what I've heard so far, you haven't missed it. Honor said she was having some troubles and things were dragging out."

Both of them sober and the tension in the air multiplies. "What kind of troubles?" Hawk snaps. "And why didn't you lead with that?"

"Easy. The last thing I heard was that once the lockdown was released on the castle, she was getting the medical care she needed. Before that, Doc, Jaxx, and Kotah were working with their hands tied behind their backs. They couldn't get her to the clinic and had no access to medical equipment."

"But that was taken care of?"

"That's what Honor said, yes."

Hawk doesn't look at all pleased and Brant's smile and easy-going mood are gone.

"The moment this is over, I'll fly you both straight back to the castle."

"Feel free to go." Mac joins the convo and hands us two FCO watches. "We found these in the guard office along with another two guards hidin' under the table. Bunch of scaredy-cat pussies if ye ask me."

I agree. "Without those collars they didn't have the juice to be big men."

Mac nods. "So, yeah, go. We've got things under control and the hostages are liberated. Yer wife and baby are more important than standin' here until things roll to a complete stop."

Hawk frowns and looks at me.

His need to get back to Calli is completely understandable. If our situations were reversed, I would be going wild to get back to Honor.

"Yeah, let me connect with my mates and make a plan. Give me a few minutes."

I leave them to watch the aftermath of the jailbreak and jog to the back of the buildings to find Dune, Tundra, and Honor. Even in the few minutes since I went to the courtyard, things have settled down almost completely at the back. I spot Tundra and Honor halfway up the incline and start hiking to join them.

"How are things at the front line?" Honor asks.

"Fine. The Elbirfae and the other squads are handling everything. Look, Hawk and Brant are anxious to get back to the castle. I told them I would fly them there without delay so they can be with Calli but I'm not sure what you guys want to do and how you want to handle things from here."

"I want to be with Calli," Honor says, looking torn, "but standing around while she gives birth does no one any good. I think I need to stay and debrief the prisoners so we can get them back into our communities first."

"That makes sense. Do you mind if I bail and leave the three of you to take care of that?"

"Not at all. In fact, I insist. Calli and I have been close for a lot of years but the bond she shares with her mates is so much more powerful. The best thing I can do for her is get them back to her as quickly as I can."

"Don't worry about us," Tundra says. "We'll take good care of our girl and meet up as soon as we can."

I extend my hand and meet Tundra with a fist bump before turning to Honor and pulling her in for a quick kiss. "Be safe, Princess. I love you."

"I love you too, magic man. Get them home and we'll join you as soon as we can."

"What? You're leaving?" Dune lands at Honor's side. "The fun is just beginning."

I nod. "No rest for the wicked, Sandman. Take good care of them while I'm gone, yeah?"

"Yeah. Will do."

CHAPTER TEN

Honor

It takes an hour after Lukas leaves before we have everyone evacuated and loaded into the buses. Many of the healthy Elbirfae choose to spread their wings and fly. After two years of having to remain beneath the grid of the prison, the freedom of soaring is too much to resist.

"Where are we headed, lass," Mac asks, as he rallies the last of the FCO enforcers into a truck.

"We have to drive at least to the Fringe and then we can take a portal to the hub in Dornte."

"We could do that, but could I offer another suggestion?" Tundra asks.

"Of course, what are you thinking, T?"

"The Amberloq compound where Valorous ruled is not far from this sector of Dornte once we get out of the Fringe and into the quadrant proper. Since the home biomes of our people have been destroyed, I suggest we go there for the temporary housing until these survivors can rebuild."

I consider his suggestion and come up with a question of my

own. "If the buildings and villages within the biomes have all been destroyed, what makes you think that Valorous's compound is intact?"

"Because we went there after we left Mount Hekko," Dune says. "From what we could tell, Laryssa and the Blood Witch used the compound once the Amberloq warriors were slaughtered."

"We think they were searching for the Amberloq Chronicles," Tundra adds. "There was evidence to support our theory that they stationed a group of people there full-time. We believe when Lukas and Creed eliminated those two women as a threat to the quadrant, whoever was stationed there left in a hurry before being discovered."

I like the sound of that.

"If it's intact and there is space enough to house these displaced citizens, that's good enough for me. While we're there, I'd like to access the Guardian's Library and see if my aunt continued her duty to record the important events during her ruling."

"I believe she did," Tundra says. "Your aunt might have done things very differently than you, but she had you in mind as her successor for much of her reign. She loved you and believed in your abilities."

"A lot of good that does me. I could've used her in my life to prepare me to take her place as the crown's protector. Instead, she left our family vulnerable to be taken prisoner and tortured."

"That's in the past," Dune says. "You're going to rule your own way and things will be different."

Tundra nods. "And now that we have representation from the third biome, your Biome General should feel the call and join us in rebuilding the Amberloq forces."

I hadn't thought of that. Another General? Six people in a mating bond? Why not keep adding men? Maybe I'll start a commune.

"When do you think he'll feel the call and join us?"

Dune and Tundra exchange a look.

"We felt it immediately," Tundra says.

"Yeah, as soon as you woke," Dune adds.

I scan the windows of the buses, trying to think of who the dominant warrior was from the Forested Jungle Biome. There were so many Elbirfae... The only person who comes to mind is the brunette who had the knife to my throat. "Where is Lark?"

Tundra scans the crowd of those standing outside the buses and points. "Over there, speaking to one of the desert elders."

She must feel our attention shift toward her because when her conversation ends, she turns her head and lifts her chin in question.

I wave for her to join us.

"Princess Thornebane, thank you for all you have done for us today."

"It's my pleasure. I know what it is to be held against your will. I was only rescued from the prison Laryssa and the Blood Witch trapped me in a few weeks ago. Dornte is a quadrant filled with citizens healing the wounds of war."

Lark nods, her emerald green eyes sharp and intelligent. "It's hard to believe it's over. When Laryssa stopped coming here to gloat, we wondered why but we had no idea she'd been killed. From what the soldiers said, it was your mate, a man from the Human Realm."

"Yes, Lukas and Creed were responsible for the deaths of both Laryssa and the Blood Witch."

"And the fae from the Human Realm formed a familial alliance with King Creed?"

I nod. "Yes. My brother was taken to the other realm by Laryssa as a show of strength. Little did she expect for him to become soul-seared to the younger sister of the fae king."

"The universe works in magical ways," Tundra says.

"It does. And that brings me to why I called you over. Who is the dominant male leader of the Forested Biome? We were beginning to think there wouldn't be a representation for a Biome General for your people. Thankfully, now, that won't be the case."

Lark takes a half step back and smiles at the people gathered. "If you're looking for a male to complete your Biome Generals, you're in for a long wait, Princess."

"Other than our elders and children, all males were slaughtered at the time of our capture. Roan is our oldest male eligible to become a Biome General and he has more than a decade of growth before he's old enough to apply to be an Amberloq warrior."

I follow the gesture of her pointing finger to the young boy who spoke to us in the barracks.

Lark is right, he's nowhere near grown enough to assume the position of the Amberloq representative for his biome. "Yes, we met earlier."

"If I may, Princess," Lark says. "Why must the Biome General be a male? Is there a law stating a female is unworthy to lead her people?"

"I don't know exactly, but I can't see why there would be. If I'm considered worthy to lead the entire Amberloq Army and its generals, why wouldn't a female be worthy to stand as a Biome General?"

"We agree on that," Lark says, bowing her head. "And since that is the case, I put my name forward for consideration. Don't mistake my confidence for arrogance. I simply know what I'm capable of. Once we are settled and you have a chance to interview the people of the Forest Biome, I invite you to hold a vote of who the people want to represent their interests."

Dune's eyebrow arches and I see his mind is rapidly freefalling into some erotic fantasy of this woman joining our mating quint.

"Not happening, Dune." I meet his gaze and shake my head. "I have no problem partnering with a female, working with a female, and becoming close friends with a female, but that's where it ends. There will be no other female in our mating bond."

Lark barks a laugh and looks at my Desert Plains General. "Agreed. I like my lovers to have deep voices and large cocks. I'm not interested in sharing a bed with another female... even if she is as beautiful and powerful as the Princess of Dornte. No offense meant."

I grin. "None taken. I feel the same way. I'm far too possessive to share my men with another woman. And since it's the Guardian of the Crown who decides the relationship she shares with the Biome Generals, I don't have to."

The crestfallen dismay on Dune's face is too funny. I roll my eyes and shoo him away, turning toward the buses. "That's something we can worry about when we get to where we're going. For now, let's get out of this place and focus on what lies ahead."

"Looking forward to it, Princess," Lark says. "The sooner we leave the better."

Shadow

"They're on their way back home," Rhylan says, bursting into the clinic waiting room. "I just got a message from Lukas. Brant and Hawk have been recovered from the detainment compound and will be here shortly. They are almost home and readying to land."

"Detainment compound?" Keyla sits up straighter in her chair and frowns. "I didn't know they had been taken."

All eyes in the room turn to me and for once I wish Moonshade wasn't so eager to meet eye contact. "Apologies. When Honor left, I knew she was escorting the FCO teams to breach a prisoner compound where they believed Hawk and Brant had been taken after the ambush. Because they didn't know what state the two of them were in, I was asked not to say anything and make things more difficult for Calli or any of you."

"But they're all right?" Jaxx asks, panic and worry weighing heavily on him.

"Definitely all right," Rhylan says. "Lukas said they are eager to get home and meet their baby girl."

Jaxx runs his fingers through his blond hair and sighs. "We'd all like to meet our baby girl."

"Calli especially," Keyla adds.

My heart goes out to our phoenix girl. The past twenty hours have not been easy on her. We hoped by moving down to the clinic and having access to the equipment she needed, things would turn around for her.

Not so. Or at least not yet.

"So, there's still no baby?" Rhylan's question is out of his mouth before he realizes what a minefield he's stepped in. When Jaxx's neck pivots and the jaguar's growl rumbles in our chests, the dragon tries to backpedal. "Sorry. I've been awake for almost forty-eight hours and have lost all sense of social cues. Forgive me."

Jaxx stands up and reclaims the circuit he's been pacing for hours.

"Sorry, Little Wolf," Rhylan says, sinking into the sofa beside Keyla's chair. "I didn't mean to pull the jaguar's tail and make things worse."

Keyla presses a palm of her hand against Rhylan's cheek. "Not your fault, sweetie. We're all tired and run ragged from the last two days. Once Brant and Hawk get here, I'm sure baby Liza will stop procrastinating. She's probably just waiting for all her daddies to be in the room before she makes her grand entrance."

"From your lips to the goddess's ears," Jaxx says, passing by on his way to the mini-fridge and then past the door before rebounding back.

It might be selfish for me to think about it, but I'm just as eager for Lukas to return as they are. Yes, it's been horribly difficult for Calli and everyone worried about the delivery, but they're not the only ones worried.

I've been worried about my mates.

All four of them were involved in the invasion of the goblin compound. If things went badly and another bomb went off, I could've lost everything.

My mates. My hopes for the future. My love.

It's all too new to feel secure in it yet.

Lukas is the one who loves me and invited me into the Thornebane Quint. Honor is precious, and I have feelings for her. But realistically, if something were to happen to either one of them, I doubt Tundra or Dune would make any effort to be part of my life.

We're just not there yet.

And we're never going to be there if we don't start spending some time in the same place at the same time without the world falling apart around us.

Not that any of that has been within our control.

The tension in the clinic has been unbearable for hours and I don't blame Moonshade when she squirms on my lap and gets restless. "Yes, sweeting. Why don't we go out to the forest for a bit and stretch our legs?"

Even the mention of going outside lifts the spirits of my little wolf cub. She went from being a wild wolf to my bound companion to being forced into a lockdown all in forty-eight hours.

I don't blame her for being stir crazy.

The nice thing about taking her for walks is that she's learning to stay at my side and walk with me. There are still moments when she's curious and looking in every direction but for the most part, we're learning to do things together.

As we navigate the halls of the castle, her focus is solely on the exit. That makes things much easier.

When we get to the exit, I nod to the two men standing guard at the door, push through the heavy, wooden door, and follow my girl out onto the cobbled patio area.

Moonshade is quick to run toward the trees and, in a moment, she will start to explore and my vision will be skewed. I hurry to sit on the closest bench, so I don't lose my way and end up falling on my face.

It will be easier to see out of her eyes as she grows older and more mature.

Right now, everything in this world is so exciting.

I sit on the bench and turn until the breeze blows against my face. It is early evening, and the sun is almost fully descended. The warmth of the day is waning, and the chill of the night will soon be clawing its way across my skin. Until that happens, I'm determined to enjoy myself.

It's peaceful here.

I close my eyes, thankful for my many blessings.

Yes, the activation of my Oracle side makes life more difficult, but in some ways it simplified things. Before I lost my sight, I don't remember the last time I sat and listened to nature while the breeze caressed my face.

"There's the man I'm looking for."

I smile up at the darkness, Lukas's accent a welcome balm to my weary soul. "I'm hoping you mean me," I say smiling toward where I heard his voice. "Being blind, you might be talking to someone else, and I wouldn't even know they were here."

Lukas chuckles. "That would be pretty cheeky of me to flirt with someone else within earshot of my mate."

"You're a pretty cheeky guy."

"I am, but not when it comes to lovers. In the life partner department, I'm rock solid and devoted. You're stuck with me, I'm afraid." Lukas's hand is warm on my jaw as he leans in. "Fuck, I missed you."

Warm lips brush over mine and I groan as my body responds. Pressing me into the back of the bench, I sense his strength is barely restrained. He claims my mouth as if I offer him refuge from the storm we've all been weathering.

I smile up at him. "I love that you missed me. In fact, I was sitting here praising the Powers for bringing you safely home. I'm assuming the others are well and with you?"

"Everyone is fine, though sadly, they're not with me. We liberated close to three hundred Elbirfae at that fucking compound. The others are taking them to the Amberloq compound where Tundra and Dune were stationed before the raids."

"Are we waiting for them to return here?"

"No plan yet. If they're coming back here, we'll wait, otherwise, we'll go join them."

Moonshade hears Lukas's voice and comes running. The joy she feels at seeing him makes my heart flutter. She adores him almost as much as I do.

Through her eyes, I see how his face lights up as he sees her. It's a joy to see him so happy. He looks tired. Yes, well, everyone is tired.

"What do you say, little one? Do you think I could convince your bonding partner to join me for a change of scenery?"

"What do you have in mind?"

He holds the wolf up to his face and winks at me. "Would you care to take my arm and go for a walk through the forested paths?"

"We would love that, but should we stay close by until after Calli has given birth?"

His smile falters as he shifts Moonshade to cradle her in his arms so she stops licking his face. "I thought for sure that would be over with by the time we arrived."

"Things are not going well."

"Like, normal not going well or we should be seriously worried not going well?"

"I don't know. Moonshade and I have been trying to be supportive but honestly, all we wanted to do was go back to Amberloq Hall and spend quiet time being out of their way."

He takes my hand and wraps our arms together, pulling me into motion. "That's perfectly understandable. You're going through a big change yourself. I don't think anyone would fault you for stepping away for a few hours."

I wave away his concern. "What stopped us wasn't fear of being judged but that we weren't sure whether Amberloq Hall has been cleared for us to return. Breard's rebels invaded the mansion during the raid. The FCO enforcers went to evict them, but no one mentioned if we can go home."

Lukas squeezes my hand and pulls me to a stop. I'm not sure why until we're chest-to-chest and his lips are brushing mine again. This kiss isn't as strong and desperate as our first.

This one is soft and slow.

"It's a big turn-on for me when you say things like that, Shadow."

I swallow, tilting my head back as his kiss shifts across my jaw. "Things like what?"

"You just called Amberloq Hall our home. Is that how you think of it?"

"Of course. That's where we're building our life, right?" I gasp as his hands slide into my hair and he brushes the peaks of my ears. "That's where Honor needs to be. And where she is... we are."

"Yeah, that's how I see it."

"Then it's home. Where the two of you are is where I want to be. It doesn't matter to me if it's in a castle or a mansion or a cave in the side of a mountain. I'm there."

A cool breeze whips past us and I'm reminded that we're not somewhere private. We're in the forested paths of the Thornebane grounds and we're the mates of the princess. If someone were to see us...

"Is it wrong that all I want is to be naked?"

"Not in my book." Demanding fingers grip the fasteners of my pants and then Lukas is pushing the fabric down my thighs. "If you need to anchor yourself, there's a wide trunk of an oak a half step behind you or a sapling to grab with your right hand."

A chill races up my spine as the cool night air hits my heated flesh... and that's before he drops down before me and his hot mouth sucks in my cock.

"Sweet mercies." My hips thrust forward and gasp as he takes me fully into his mouth. Thrown off-balance, I spear my arm out to the side to grab that sapling. "Are you sure we should be doing this? Right here? Right now?"

Lukas's husky chuckle is all male and all hunger. "Oh, yeah. It has to be right now, or I think I might die."

CHAPTER ELEVEN

Lukas

S hadow is too much. Here we are tucked away in the splendor of the Thornebane forest, horny as hell, hot and hungry for one another and he's worried about propriety. Cute. I could tell him I've already cast a veil of privacy and have Moonshade enclosed in our bubble, but why?

I think I'll let him enjoy the thrill of voyeurism and being discovered for a bit.

In fact… I think I'll increase it.

Easing my head back, I pop off the end of his cock and look up his body from where I'm kneeling. I push his shirt up his ribs and take in the lean musculature of my elf. "Didn't you say something about being naked?"

"What? Here?"

"Oh yeah. We're about to get *au naturale* in nature. Take everything off and I'll do the same." It's a shame to abandon his erection if even for a moment, but clothes must come off. I pull the buckles of my boots and toe them off. Next go my gun holster, shirt, pants, and boxers. By the time I'm tossing my

Calvins onto the pile, Shadow is gloriously bare. "Damn, you're stunning in the light of the first moon."

Shadow laughs. "That's quite a pickup line, soldier. How does it usually work for you?"

"It's the first time I've tried it. I'll report back later and tell you how it went."

His smile is warm and trusting and I step forward to bring our bodies together. When I stroke my hands down his chest and over the muscled ridges of his abs, goosebumps raise his skin. "Are you cold?"

"No. It's not that."

I rub my hands up and down his arms and make sure he's telling the truth. It's not cold out here but in the shadows of the forest, as darkness is falling, it's not as warm as it was all day.

I'm pleased to feel how warm his skin is. "So, if you're not cold, what is it?"

"I missed you."

I pull him tighter into my embrace and wrap my arms around him. Chest against chest. Hips against hips. Thighs against thighs. It's incredibly arousing to simply be standing here naked with him in my arms. "I missed you too. I love you, by the way. Did I mention that?"

"No. I had no idea."

He's teasing me and I thrust my hips forward, increasing the friction in all the most delicious places. "You know, I've always appreciated a great blowjob—"

"As one does."

"Exactly… but I'm thinking no one has ever rung in with their opinion about whether or not I *give* a great blowjob."

"And you neglected to give out comment cards afterward to gauge the level of satisfaction from your male lovers?"

"I must have. Honestly, as confident as I am in my skills with a woman, I haven't had many male partners so there might be room to up my game."

"I doubt that. You are a gifted lover."

"No. I think you should let me practice my moves and weigh in with your thoughts. I'm aiming for the greatest blowjob ever. If you like, I can even make up some comment cards."

Shadow laughs and reaches out to grab hold of the small tree beside us. "I agree to the experiment. Do with me as you wish. Show me your moves."

I tilt my head and look at the ground behind him. Raising my hand, I call forward a little nature magic and make us a nice little mossy patch on the ground. "It's tough to truly enjoy an orgasm standing up. How about we get a little more comfortable?"

Shadow chuckles. "Maybe you should have thought about that before we got undressed in the middle of the forest. I'm all for nature but pointy sticks and bugs that bite my bits aren't on my list of turn-ons."

I chuckle and lead him back the three steps before easing him down to lay with me. "Nothing a little magic won't fix. Now, lay back and enjoy."

He relaxes into the mossy nest I made us and smiles up at the stars he can't see.

Damn, he steals my heart.

Lowering myself beside him, I prop up on my elbow and rest my free hand on the beautiful landscape of his body. In a slow, gentle circuit, I run my touch from the tightened peak of his nipple, down the rippled plains of his abs, and teasingly close to the eager erection bobbing against his navel, hoping for attention. "So, what *is* on your list of turn-ons?"

He closes his eyes and smiles. "Well, you mentioned aiming for the greatest blowjob of all time. I think we should start working toward that. It takes a great deal of training to be awarded a title of true excellence."

"I like the way you think." I begin to slide my way down the side of his body when I pause, remembering his hesitation earlier. "By the way, feel free to get vocal. We're in our own little private world out here. I've cast the spell to ensure our privacy."

"I figured as much. I couldn't imagine you would risk our frivolity negatively impacting Honor."

I chuckle, getting back to my travels down his body. "Frivolity? I like the sound of that. All right, let's get my first attempt at the world's greatest blowjob started."

"Yes. Let's."

It takes me a moment to get my bearings. After all the stroking and talking I lost a bit of my focus. Although, with a man like Shadow naked and waiting for me to devour him, it's easy to reignite the inspiration.

Draping myself over his hip, I use the hand I was exploring with to lift his arousal as I lick my lips and take him into my mouth. His hips rise to thrust further, and I shift my grip to fondle the sensitive orbs in his sac.

He groans. "Oh, a good start."

I chuckle around the silky steel of his cock and focus on making him feel good. Up and down his length I slide, my head rising and falling in a slow and deliberate bob. When I get to the tip, I slide my tongue through the small slit at the tip of his weeping crown.

The unique taste of his essence calls to something dark and possessive within me. He is mine.

Mine to protect. Mine to pleasure. Mine to love.

The afternoon we spent at Amberloq Hall committing ourselves to one another seems like weeks or months ago... not days.

How can I need him so desperately after such a short time? Is that even normal? Maybe the magic of fae bonding is at work here too. I believe that.

Because the passion and desire I feel when I'm like this with Shadow isn't a choice—it's a carnal need.

Another groan.

Time to raise the bar. I pop off the tip and swallow, shifting my hold from his balls so that I can stroke him through his release. I breathe deep, the sight of what I'm doing to him searing me.

I could lose it just by getting him off.

Gripping him tighter, I continue to pump my hand and increase the pressure.

"Yes," he hisses. "Mercy that feels good."

I watch how his body undulates, his breathing growing quick and shallow. The moon is out above and the silvery light is glistening across his bare skin.

I give him a session of fast fisting and then get back to sucking his cock. There is that taste again. I suck harder, squeezing as I stroke, milking him so that drops of cum leak out for me to savor.

I lap them up.

But as much as I love drinking him down, this is *his* blowjob. I swipe the head of his cock with my tongue before increasing the speed of my hand and hammering him fast and hard.

I stretch on my side so that I can continue to toss him off but at the same time suck his nipple into my mouth. Gripping the tiny bud of nerves between my teeth, I give it a little pinch.

"Yes... more of that."

"Mhmm," I mumble against his flesh. You'd think my arm is getting tired but even though I am palming him like a jackhammer I could do this for hours.

The tingling in my sac is unwelcome.

I don't want this to be about me going off early. This is supposed to be me blowing his mind. Pushing back the urge to release, I focus on him.

Fuck he's hot.

With his eyes clenched shut, his stomach muscles tight, and his breathing coming in short bursts, Shadow is the image of sexy and about to orgasm.

"Gods I want to fuck you. Come hard and give me enough cream to slick you up good."

As if obeying me, his head kicks back and he spills onto his clenching abs.

Yes... this.

I don't slow down. I want him to ride this out for all it's worth. Magic tingles across my skin and there's no way I can hold it back. Shadow calls to something inside me. Honor does too. The three of us were incredible together and I wish she was here to watch Shadow come unglued like this.

As the convulsing of his pleasure eases, I swipe my fingers through the creamy mess on his abdomen and shift down his body. "If you're game, I want you."

"I want that too."

"Do you want to be on your back or your knees?"

"On my back. I like to touch you while you're taking me. You are very sexy."

"I like that too."

He pegs me with a look so hot, I almost convulse into a round of cum spurting myself.

I look at the cream glistening in my fingers and position myself for the next event. "Lift your knees."

One thing I love about Shadow is that he's agreeable to anything... and eager. So, fucking eager.

I glance down at my hips and chuckle. My cock is raging hard and demanding attention.

He's no more eager than me.

After depositing his cum right where I need it, I widen his knees and play a little to get him primed and ready. I smile as his spent cock jumps and starts to thicken for me again.

Tilting my hips, I lean in and slick the tip of my erection in the lubrication of his cum and start testing, teasing, and toying with him.

I slip my thumb past the resistance of his ass and stretch him. "Fuck, I missed you."

His hand slides down his chest and grips his arousal. "I missed you too. I don't want to sound needy or even greedy but I don't like being left behind when you guys go off to save the world."

"It's not that glamorous. I'd much rather lock myself in Amberloq Hall for the next decade solely to pleasure my mates. All naked all the time."

"I like the sound of that."

I'm trying to go slow and ease my way inside but I'm too hungry. I push through the resistance and force myself to still until the muscles squeezing me relax.

"Give yourself a little love while I watch." While he establishes a rhythm, I test his acceptance of my presence and start a slow in and out. "When we get home tonight, we're going to do this again but we'll be properly slicked, so the ride is all glide."

"No complaints, but yes, I look forward to more."

Me too. Now my mind is lighting up with all kinds of scenarios. Shadow must be doing the same thing because he's arching into my penetrations, and I pick up the pace to meet his need.

"Maybe later I'll give you a world's greatest blowjob and then bend you over and take you."

Assertive. Nice. Shadow hasn't shown any dominance yet in our bed. He's met my aggression but he's always been on the receiving end of the fucking. If he wants to step up and get his groove on, I'm willing to bend over for him.

Imagining that, my body shudders.

With his knees in the air, I open him wider and lean harder into the back of his thighs. "Then I better finish off so we can get there and give you a chance to be the star of the show."

Shadow grunts as I start ramming in earnest. The forward

thrust has my balls swinging in the open air and slapping his ass. "Too rough?"

He swallows and shakes his head. "No. It's perfect. I want you just like this... hungry and horny."

I chuckle, my release building pressure deep in my core. "Then you're in luck because I'm not just hungry... I'm famished."

Dune

The buses arrive at our old home, and Tundra and I land on the front lawn with the Elbirfae prisoners who chose to fly. There's a great deal of excitement in the air, the idea of sleeping free and safe for the first time in over two years bubbling up in squeals and laughter. This is the first day of a new life of possibility.

I remember feeling that way the day I first arrived.

As a new warrior, I was so filled with confidence and illusions of grandeur. I was fully convinced I would walk through those doors and blow everyone's mind with my superior Amberloq abilities.

It seems so stupid now.

"What seems stupid, sweetie?" Honor steps in beside me and flashes me a tired smile.

I jolt from my mental musings and look around.

Tundra is escorting a group inside and I'm standing here looking like a daft lawn ornament talking to myself. "Just reminiscing about my aspirations when I first arrived. I was so sure I would walk through those doors and make my mark. Instead, I crashed in shame."

"Not everyone is a perfect fit from the start. There's a learning curve. Look at me. I'm certainly not the Amberloq

General I thought I'd be. It's not too late for us. I have every intention of turning things around and taking the quadrant by storm."

Maybe she's right. Maybe I'm not hopeless.

When she slides her arm around my hip, I reach across her back and pull her against my side. "You look so tired, Princess."

"I am. I need to get everyone settled here so we can get home to Calli, Lukas, and Shadow. I need to be there for her and the baby. I want to check on our home and make sure the library isn't damaged and the Chronicle Discs are still intact. I want to take a long bath and sleep for three days."

"Then off ye go, lass," Mac says, stopping as he passes by. He hands a duffle to one of the other FCO officers and turns to give us his full attention. "The fierce brunette with the ebony wings and I can get everyone bedded down and fed. Go see about yer friend and take a moment. We'll be here when ye get back."

"Oh, I can't do that. It's my job to—"

"To see yer citizens are safe. Ye've done that. Now, off ye go. Ye look like death warmed over. Go replenish the well."

"Really? You don't mind?"

The red-headed man waves a hand and laughs. "Away with ye, Princess. We'll see ye in a day or two and not a moment sooner. Have yer men draw yer bath, and give ye a foot rub, and then tuck ye in for a long-deserved sleep. These folks won't mind spendin' a day or two adjustin' to freedom. I'm sure they'll visit their homes and start plannin' how to rebuild. Lots to keep them busy for a few days."

"Bless you, Mac."

The soldier recommences his approach toward Valorous's Amberloq Hall and waves over his head. "Och, I've been blessed my whole life lass, but I thank ye for the thought."

Honor chuckles and lays her head on my shoulder. "I'm

going to lay on the grass. You go find Tundra and tell him we're going home. I'm all guardianed out. Wake me when it's time to leave."

CHAPTER TWELVE

Honor

$\mathcal{I}$ wake to the warm swipes of a tongue against my mouth and the sensual brushing of softness against my cheeks. It's disorienting but not unpleasant. The drugging pull of exhaustion doesn't want to release me from its hold, but I fight to rise to consciousness.

"Moonshade, no. Don't wake her sweeting."

Moonshade? I crack one eye open and chuckle. "Not the sensual awakening I thought I was getting."

Shadow stands over me fresh from the shower. He's bare-chested, and his hide pants are hanging enticingly low on his hips. "Apologies, we meant to let you sleep uninterrupted until you woke up naturally."

I stretch and realize two things immediately. One, my muscles are incredibly stiff. Two, if the little wolf hadn't woken me up, I may have peed the bed.

"Hold that thought." I flip back the blankets and dash for the washroom.

When I've emptied my bladder and washed up, I splash cold

water on my face and brush my teeth. Man, I've got the worst case of cottonmouth ever. Well… not ever. The worst case was when I awoke from my coma. This is a close second. "How long have I been asleep?"

"The better part of three days."

"Three days!" I practically choke on my toothpaste and have to do a quick spit and rinse. "I can't sleep for three days. Calli's in labor and I told Connor Mac I'd be back to help with the Elbirfae."

Shadow's leaning on the doorframe watching me. He looks as calm and serene as always. How does he do that? "Calli is no longer in labor. She successfully gave birth to the baby phoenix two days ago. There were a great many complications, but she is a phoenix and has risen as strong as ever."

"And baby Liza is healthy and well?"

"Baby Ashborn is healthy and well, yes."

"Ashborn? What happened to Liza?"

Lukas chuckles coming in behind Shadow and winks. "When the deal was done and Jaxx was holding a little boy, they decided Liza would just be mean."

I chuckle. "Yeah. It would be the Boy Named Sue all over again.

"Exactly. So, they decided since he was a phoenix born of the ashes… Ashborn was more appropriate. They're using Ash for his everyday name."

"Nice. I can't wait to meet him."

"They're all still guests in the King's Tower so, you've got time. Calli wouldn't head back to Pennsylvania until she saw you and you saw the babe."

"Well good. I want to see the little guy before he goes back to be the young prince of the Human Realm."

I meet the two of them at the door and hug first Shadow and then Lukas. "What else did I miss? How are the Elbirfae adjusting?"

"Very well," Dune says, striding in from the hall. "Tundra and I have kept in close contact with them, and Lark is handling things when we're not there."

I look around at our suite and smile at my dresser and belongings against the wall and the matching dresser from Creed's old room there as well.

Lukas was using that one.

Stepping into the closet, I grin at all the clothes. There are the collared shirts that Lukas wears, the soft tunic-style shirts that Shadow wears, and the pieced shirts all Elbirfae wear to account for their wings.

Those flap over their heads like a sport pinny and then zip or button up under their arms.

"You've been busy. It looks like we live here now."

Lukas nods. "We do. The five of us are officially moved in together. We brought your things from the heir's suite and made ourselves at home. Dune and Tundra collected their personal belongings from the other hall and Shadow had his stuff sent over from the castle yesterday. This is us."

Wow. That's something.

"That's all right, yes?" Shadow asks, shifting Moonshade to face me. "Your intention is still to move forward and become a family, right?"

I get a handle on my surprise and push it down. "Yes, that's right. We are. I have no doubts about what I want and need us to be. This is wonderful. I am excited to see how the next chapter of our lives unfolds."

Lukas winks, reaching out to squeeze my hand. "That's what we thought too. Now, do you want to shower and then eat or the other way around?"

"Who all is here?"

"Just us," Dune says. "Tundra went to check in with Rhylan, but he should be back soon. Until then, just the four of us."

"Then definitely eat before showering. I'm starving. It's like I slept three days or something."

Lukas lays a heavy arm across my shoulders and turns me toward the bedroom. "Or something."

Tundra

"And now that Clarinta and Travon are on board," Rhylan says, "we need to decide what type of currency we want and where to produce it."

Hawk grins. "Neutral ground, Dragon. That's the only way this will work. I've brokered enough deals with competing races and governments to know that despite best intentions, ego and mistrust always creeps into the best-laid plans."

"So, StoneHaven," Creed says. "If each quadrant has one representative overseeing the currency production and distribution, that should keep things honest, right?"

Hawk nods. "That's the idea. The only change I'd make is to appoint a representative from StoneHaven as well. Otherwise, you have four equal votes and could find yourselves in a stalemate situation. Adding the fifth means you won't get deadlocked if there are differing opinions on things."

Creed nods. "All right. The Chancellor of the StoneHaven Historical Society can be included. Kaytee is an honorable and strong woman. I can't see her being swayed by the corruption and greed we're weeding out."

My watch vibrates against my wrist, and I read the incoming text at the same time Hawk raises his wrist and does the same.

Hawk's face breaks into a wide grin. "Sorry boys, my baby boy just woke up and it's my turn to change him and watch Calli feed him. I don't want to miss my window."

Rhylan laughs. "You have to take turns watching him feed?"

"Calli put us on probation. She said the four of us are crowding her and making her crazy. Until we calm down, we've been put on restricted access. When either of them is asleep, we can all hold him and watch him as much as we want but when she's awake and doing anything with the baby, we need to cool it."

We all laugh at his expense.

"I'm on my way out too," I say. "Honor has finally woken and wants to have our first meal with all five of us together. So much has happened so quickly we've yet to all be in the same room as mates."

"That's important," Creed says, chuckling. "It's hard to be a quint if you've never all been together."

"And let me tell you from experience," Hawk says, waggling his brows. "Things will get much more interesting when the five of you all get together."

"Ugh… that's my sister, Hawk," Creed says, making a face and waving us both toward the door. "Tundra, go make Honor happy. Tell her I'd like to share a meal with her myself and catch up sometime soon."

"Maybe we can host something before Calli and the phoenix family go back to Pennsylvania," Rhylan says.

"Great idea," Creed says. "Let's make that happen."

I dip my chin and step backward. "Thank you, sire. I shall tell her."

Creed laughs. "You're mated to my sister, Tundra. You need to stop calling me sire."

"Yes, majesty. I'll work on that."

Creed laughs harder. "Yeah, you do that."

Honor

By the time Tundra gets back to the house, Lukas and I have a pub food feast ready to plate. As the princess of the quadrant, it was required of me to work many laborer jobs in the city. My skills came in handy when I assumed the body of a junkie and played the part of a street rat in the human realm. Calli and I busted our butts as servers in any restaurant or diner that would hire us.

"Here's to the Thornebane Quint," I say, holding up my beer to toast. "We may have had a rocky start, but it taught us to work past conflict and heated tempers. What happened is done. From this point on, our future lies ahead of us."

"Here's to looking forward," Lukas says.

"To building a new family," Shadow adds.

"To rebuilding what was lost so that it stands stronger than ever," Tundra says.

"And to all the hot and heavy delights that come with a five-person union."

Tundra rolls his eyes. "Really, that's what you got out of this?"

Dune shrugs, a devilish grin spreading across his face. "It needed to be said. The future stuff and the rebuilding stuff is good too, but it's going to be the personal relationships and our bonding as a five-way couple that gives us the strength to last."

I lift my glass a little higher. "He's not wrong. Intentions are all well and good, but it's our commitment to this relationship that will make us a great team moving forward."

Lukas lifts his glass and chinks it against mine. "To being a five-way couple. I'm sure it won't always go smoothly, but it's bound to be interesting."

"It'll never be boring," Dune adds.

Tundra looks at him and shakes his head. "With you in the mix, there's no chance of it being boring."

Dunes smile grows wider. "Are you flirting with me, Iceman?

Because we're bonded now, you don't have to play coy. If you want a piece of me, you can just say so."

Tundra almost chokes on his ale. He sets his glass down and dabs his napkin against his face. "I wasn't flirting with you. Only you could take that and make it sexual. I was implying you are a pain in the ass."

"One man's insult is another man's pickup line."

I laugh and get back to my burger. "Fill me in on what I missed. I can't believe you let me sleep three days. With so much going on, you should've woke me."

Lukas reaches across the table to scoop up some more potato wedges. "Yes, a lot was going on but nothing we had any control over. If there had been an event or decision to be made that affected you or your responsibilities, we would've woken you."

"In the meantime," Tundra says, "we kept an eye on things and you were able to catch up on some much-needed rest."

"But my little phoenix baby is two days old, and I've never even seen him."

Dune swallows and sets his burger down. "I'm not an expert on babies or anything, but I don't think he'll remember whether or not you were there right at the firing of the gun."

"No, definitely not," Shadow adds.

With my attention on the handsome elf of our union, I notice something is off with his mental grid. As a mind guardian, I'm very sensitive to the brain waves and mental energies of the people around me. If I hadn't known Shadow before, it wouldn't raise my attention, but knowing him as I do, the change is concerning.

Still, this is our first meal together as mates and I don't want to ruin it. When we first discovered Shadow was an Oracle, Dune reacted badly toward having him stay with us.

The last thing I want to do is ignite a spark of contention during our first peaceful moment of the five of us getting along.

No. I want to enrich the moment. Talking about what I missed is important but like they said. They've taken care of things and nothing is looming that needs my immediate attention.

"You know what? I say we shut out the world for a couple of hours. I'll send Calli a text that I'm awake and need to catch up here and then will be over to see her. Barring a military strike on the quadrant, I call a mate moment. Two hours of uninterrupted us time. Who's with me?"

A chaotic round of affirmations come back at me.

"Good, then if we agree, I say we leave the dishes for later and the five of us go upstairs to the lounge and spend a bit of time relaxing together."

"That sounds like a great idea," Lukas says.

"Your brother mentioned wanting to have us for dinner before the Phoenix Quint goes back to the Human Realm," Tundra says. "Shall I send him a response? If everyone is expecting us there in a few hours, they might not interrupt in the meantime."

"Sound logic, Tundra." I tap Shadow's hand and take it to walk him upstairs. "Please do that. Ask him to tell Calli I'm looking forward to seeing her and her baby boy. I have a bit of mate business to take care of first."

I can't help but giggle when I see the grin on Dune's face. "Yes, Dune. By mate business, I mean sex."

His grin expands and he rushes around the table to get everyone up and moving toward the door. "Finally we get to the good stuff. The whole partners in life and battle stuff is good, but I can't be the only one who's looking forward to getting our grind on."

"That's poetic," Shadow says.

Lukas laughs. "You're not the only one, Dune, but it's not like we've been procrastinating."

The five of us and Moonshade climb the wraparound staircase to the second floor, then up to the third, and then up to the lounge inside the door to our suite.

"So, not to be indelicate or anything, but how do we do this?" I ask. "Who takes the lead? Who puts what where? I've never had so many body parts to wonder about during sex before."

Lukas chuckles. "I don't know that any of us have."

"Speak for yourself, magic man," Dune says. "My people are very open and welcoming of sharing. For once, I might be the most qualified person in the room."

Lukas holds up his hands in surrender. "All right. Then, by all means, enlighten us. How do you want to handle our first time together?"

Dune grins. "Since we just ate, I think we should sit for a few minutes and get to know each other's tastes and skills." He gestures toward one of the couches and we follow his lead. "For example, we all want to be involved with Honor, that's a given, but what else do you enjoy? What are you good at? And most importantly, what are you most looking forward to?"

I decide to get us started. "I love to orgasm and am looking forward to watching the male/male action. I find it super hot to be a voyeur with you guys."

Dune grins. "Then you're in luck because we outnumber you four to one. Unless, of course, you want to reconsider Lark joining us. That would open up other avenues and shift the odds."

I bark a laugh. "Not happening. I told you that."

Dune shrugs. "Can't blame a guy for trying. Okay, true confessions. Who's next?"

Lukas raises two fingers. "Shadow and I have spent a fair bit of time together over the past three days while Tundra and Dune were tending to the Elbirfae. T and I have been dancing around a few plans of things we'd like to do together. I'd like to start there and, of course, make my way back to sex up Honor."

"That works for me," Tundra says. "Lukas and I have some promises to keep. After that, I'd like to get to know Shadow better. And, of course, make my way back to sexing up Honor, too."

"Excellent," Dune says. "So, Lukas and Tundra can start acting out their fantasies while Shadow and I give Honor the orgasms she's looking for. Then, we'll adjust accordingly. Sound good?"

I press a hand against my racing heart. Now that the moment is here, I've got butterflies. "Sounds perfect. If you boys don't mind, I'd like to start in the shower. I slept for three days and ran around defending the castle for a day and a half before that. I need a shower. I wouldn't object to someone sudsing me up."

Dune grins at Shadow. "It's a good thing the Guardian's suite has a massive shower. I have a feeling we're going to be using it a lot."

Shadow returns the smile. "Proper daily hygiene is very important."

"Good point, Counselor. The shower is a great place to start."

CHAPTER THIRTEEN

Honor

𝒶 mberloq Hall has stood as the home for the Thornebane Guardian of the Crown for centuries. Four men with one woman to lead them. It was the way of things until my aunt became the guardian. The beauty of returning to that tradition is that the size of the royal suite and the ensuite is based on five people living in one space.

Some ancestor of mine renovated this place and had the foresight to install a five-person shower built in the master ensuite. It has adjustable jet sprayers, ledges to lean over, benches to sit on or prop up a foot, and all manner of strategically placed handles to make use of.

I intend to make good use of them.

The entire setup is built for group sex shenanigans and at this moment, I'm praising their foresight. Because, even though Lukas and Tundra want to explore a little on their own first, they say they'll join us in a bit.

I'm looking forward to that. "Since I'm the only one of us who's been naked with each of you, I'll go first."

The first thing I do is snap my fingers and get Moonshade's attention, and then I bite my lip and make a seductive show out of sliding my clothes off. I tease a little, wriggling my hips as I slink my shirt up my ribs.

Since this is what I slept in for three days, there's no bra to remove. It's me wearing my undies and my boyfriend's t-shirt.

That's how I roll.

When I'm naked, I tug the elastic off the end of my braid and free the woven plaits with my fingers. As I rake my hair loose, Shadow and Dune both shuck off their clothes.

The bathroom floor quickly becomes a heap of discarded fabric and then the three of us are naked. When Moonshade climbs up onto the clothes, tromps in a circle, and lays down, I take Shadow's hand and lead him toward the shower.

"Dune, if you don't mind, can you get us set up?"

"My pleasure."

My desert representative reaches in and taps an electronic control panel which activates a program for the front and back nozzles. There's no denying that Dune naked and taking charge is a great look for him.

Glancing over, I watch the muscles in his back flex and tighten as he walks to get the towels. His wings sway behind him as the tight globes of his ass dimple. It's as if he was sculpted by one of the great Renaissance masters.

"Michelangelo couldn't have done better."

He turns his head, his turquoise eyes alive with mischief. "What's that, Princess?"

I chuckle. "Oh, I think you heard me. I said the carved lines of your body are perfection. The one time we were together, we were horizontal and I didn't get to admire the view. This is nice for me."

He returns with an armload of terry towels and then faces me, giving me a full-frontal view before flaring his tan and brown wings and doing a slow runway turn. "Feel free to ogle. I'm not shy."

No, he's not. And by the way his cock is hardening, he likes to be looked at. "For Shadow's benefit, let's move from the visual stimulation into the realm of tactile seductions. Let's play a little game of you wash my front and I'll wash yours."

Shadow chuckles. "I like what you did there."

"Yeah? I did too… because as nice as backs are, I want to be touching your fronts."

"Then come inside," Dune says, ducking behind the foggy glass wall. "The water is fine."

You don't have to ask me twice.

Running a gentle caress down the front of Shadow's body, I take hold of his erection and tug him forward to lead him into the shower. He sets a steadying hand on my shoulder and chuckles. "That is my leash, is it?"

"Any objections?"

"None. You have free reign to claim any part of my body and soul you wish to possess. I am yours for the taking."

"That's good to know. Watch your step. There's a four-inch lip to keep the water of the shower from running onto the floor. You'll need to step… yep, you've got it."

He steps up and over the low obstacle without issue and then we've arrived. Circling behind me, Shadow presses against my ass and shifts until we're under the spray. The water is warm, and I groan as it hits my chest and runs down my breasts.

"Gods this feels good." Yeah, I need this.

Shadow's hands slide around my ribs and across my navel. "Dune, can you help me with the soap?"

"Sure can," he says, grabbing a beige bar off the ledge and bringing it over. He turns it over in his wet hands, bringing his palms to a lather before surrendering it to our elf. "I think you were right about that daily hygiene regimen, Counselor. I think we should start every day like this."

"No objection." Shadow shifts behind me, his arousal hard and pressed against the small of my back. When his soapy palms cross my body and start washing me, I drop my head back and soak in the sensation.

"That feels amazing."

"It's pretty amazing to watch, too," Dune says. He's standing directly in front of me, running his sudsy hands over his pecs and down to his groin.

Wow.

Water cascading down his bare flesh is hella sexy.

He tugs on his cock and I groan. He's got a firm grip and when he strokes himself, his mental energy is so provocative it sends a rush of cream to my core.

Shadow's hands are exploring my front. His fingers glide over the wet sheen on my skin until one hand pauses on my nipple and the other drops down to my core. With a probing middle finger, he slides into my heat and finds the tight nerves of my clit.

"How about Dune and I help you release some of the tension of the past week. You said you enjoy a good orgasm, correct?" His fingers delve between my legs.

I buck as he tweaks my clit and my right nipple at the same time. His assertion is a nice surprise. When we were together with Lukas, he was tentative. Not so now.

Is that because he's feeling more secure in this mating or because he doesn't feel submissive with Dune here instead of Lukas?

I suppose time will answer that.

The air in the shower has become humid and my muscles are starting to relax. Man, I'm sore. Between the raid on the castle and then the compound and then sleeping for days, my muscles have had it rough.

"Are you falling asleep on us, Princess?" Dune asks, arching a brow.

"Not even a little." I swallow, watching him stroke himself in front of me. "Just reveling in the bliss of the moment."

"Bliss is good." He steps closer, reaches down with his free hand, and lifts one of my legs to rest it on a ledge a foot off the ground. "Open up and give Shadow more access to the goods."

I'm good with that. In fact, I'm great.

Shadow fingers me more ardently and tightens his hold across my ribs. His cock grinds against my ass and I rub against him. "I want you inside me, Shadow. From behind, right where you are."

Shadow eases his hips back and then the crown of his erection probes at my core. I bend forward to give him access and then he's filling me.

"Yes." I gasp arching back against his hold. My pussy stretches and adjusts to his presence. Shadow is very aroused and because of that, deliciously hard. "You feel wonderful, Shadow."

"So, slecking hot." Dune increases the speed of his stroking. He's going to lose it. His breathing is fast and his expression is all about sexual release.

I groan, grab his wing and pull him closer. "You're too far away."

"Just letting off a little sexual steam while Shadow primes you. I want to last as long as possible when it's my turn to be inside you."

"Then stroke off and make a mess of me. I want your cum all over my front while Shadow takes me from the back."

Before he can say anything, I close my fingers in his hair and pull his mouth to mine. Claiming his kiss, I sweep my tongue into his mouth and focus on the climax building at my core.

These men are breathtaking.

It's a sexual game of Honor In The Middle and I love it. The steady rocking rhythm to Dune's shoulder muscles tells me he's stroking off hard and fast. He breaks away from our kiss and arches back gasping for air as creamy streams of cum hit my navel.

Shadow penetrates me from behind and rubs my clit at the same time. He's driving me crazy.

Dune's hands smear through his mess, spreading his release up my ribs and over my breasts. "Lean forward, beautiful. I'll hold you up so Shadow can get some solid leverage behind you."

I do as he asks and the shift in position is too much. A few strong thrusts and then my reality detonates and my body shatters. I shout out, my cries echoing against the hard tile surfaces.

Dune holds me as my body convulses and my inner muscles grip and squeeze. Shadow slows a little, giving me a moment to focus on the sensations and ride out my release. The friction of in and out is sexy as hell—the sound of his body slamming home even better.

With him deep inside me, I open up my senses to them fully and my knees threaten to give out.

Dune keeps me from falling and chuckles. "Don't get weak in the knees yet. Our boy here is about to—yep, here he goes."

Shadow's steady in and out loses its rhythm as he grunts and his hips lock. His hands grip my hips with bruising force as he holds me in place and shatters behind me. His orgasm is violent but beautiful and when his body relaxes, he folds over onto my back.

The rapid pounding of his heart beats against my spine. It takes a moment for him to catch his breath and then he seems to realize he's still inside me. "Apologies, I must be heavy."

I chuckle. "No, but it's a little odd being bent over like this."

He grunts and forces himself to straighten. "Sorry about that."

"Oh, no, don't be." I try to get up but need help from Dune. Once I'm standing straight, Dune steps out of the way and pulls me under the spray. "You're messier than you were when you came in here."

The water is warm and Dune's hands are gentle as he rinses off my belly and thighs. I'm not sure if it's the orgasms, the heat in the air, or the emotion of being with these two men, but I'm light-headed.

"There." Dune finishes with the post-sex cleanup and turns off the water. "How are you feeling now?"

"Wonderful, thank you."

"Good. Let's get you dried off. Round two will be on our bed. I don't think our legs will take another stand-up session."

Shadow chuckles. "Agreed."

Dune

If this is my life, I won't complain. Naked and with a towel wrapped around my hips, I escort Honor and Shadow back to our massive bed, strategizing about how the next round of mate bonding sex will unfold. Tundra and Lukas are laying in the afterglow of their orgasms and I shoo them over to make room.

"All went well with you two?" I ask, even though the answer is obvious.

"Very well indeed." Lukas is stretched out with the sheet draped across his muscled thigh and his body glistening. I find his confidence attractive—as well as him lying there naked.

Lukas knows who he is and doesn't doubt it.

That's hot.

I tear my ogling away and shift my gaze to Tundra. He's lying on his side, grinning. "No complaints here."

I'm glad. For years the two of us have been coming together and afterward, there's been nothing but hostility and regrets. It's nice that he can smile afterward with Lukas. It's a slap to my ego, but today's a new day.

Maybe we'll get there too.

"So, what's next," Lukas asks, gesturing to the three of us. "You're the party planner, Dune. Have at it."

Right. I get back into the moment. "For the next phase of mate bonding, I'd like to be balls deep inside Honor and have my retinas burned out by an indecent amount of naked down-and-dirty by you boys."

Lukas chuckles. "Okay then. Our iceman said he wants some Shadow time, so if everyone is still agreeable, Tundra, this is Shadow. Shadow, Tundra. Be sure to burn Dune's retina's out."

Tundra gets up and rounds the end of the bed to drape an arm over Shadow's shoulder. "We'll do our best but I meant what I said. Shadow and I don't know each other overly well. I'm looking to build some bonds, not just get indecent with him."

"Look at you protecting his honor," I say, laughing. "You overthink things, Frosty. Sometimes naked and having fun is enough. But hey, you do you and I'll do these two. No problem."

Shadow doesn't look like he has any reservations about spending naked time with Tundra. From what I've heard about elves, they're just as accepting of lovers as my people are. I'm sure they'll figure it out.

I grin at Lukas and Honor. "And then there were three. So, what's our plan?"

Lukas smiles. "Didn't you say you want to be balls deep in Honor?"

"I do, yeah."

"Well, then, I guess I'll take the back seat and be balls deep in you while you're balls deep in her."

I'm not sure I was offering to give Lukas the dominant position over me, but I just finished telling Tundra to stop overthinking things.

Right. Sometimes naked and having fun is enough.

"Okay, magic man, that'll work. But you've got to give me a

few minutes with Honor first. I want to drive the train for a bit before I'm the one getting driven."

Lukas nods. "That's fair. Come here, babe. Let me get my hands on you. I missed you the past few days."

Honor drops her towel and goes to him without hesitation. There's a gleam in her eyes when she's with Lukas that isn't there yet with the rest of us.

She loves him.

The reality of that hits me like a right cross to the jaw. That's what *I* want. I want her to love me. I want her to light up when I call her to the bed so I can have sex with her.

No, not just sex. I want to make love to her.

My mind replays memories of the morning we woke up in the same bed and got together. That wasn't sex. That was her and I coming together with slow hands and languid thrusts. It was wonderful.

That's what Honor deserves in a lover.

I guess, we all deserve that.

"Everything okay, sweetie?" Honor looks up at me with a quizzical gaze.

I shake my head and bark a laugh. "Yeah, sorry. Just distracted by personal growth and all that."

She grins. "Well, if it helps, I think your personal growth is going very well. It's been a pleasure to be around you the past couple of days."

The smile she flashes me is warm and honest. It's not the gushing love that Lukas got, but I guess I haven't earned that level of affection yet.

But I will.

CHAPTER FOURTEEN

Honor

The afternoon sexy times with the five of us is wonderful and at the end of two hours, I think we've all grown a lot closer. I know it could be the sex, but I feel like it's deeper than that. Dune's taken great strides at not making us want to punch his face. Shadow and Tundra are getting closer. And I'm optimistic the five of us can get on the same page.

After another quick shower—alone this time—I get dressed and meet the guys downstairs. They're all milling around in the open concept living room with their coats on, so I grab my boots from the front hall and bring them in to sit down and lace-up.

"So, what else did I miss? Am I up to date?"

"Not really," Lukas says. "You got the highlights before the sexual distraction but it's been busy."

"Okay, then fill me in."

Tundra takes the lead on the conversation and tells me about the progress on stabilizing the quadrant's currency. "Given that the physical strike of Ruic Breard's goblin rebellion failed, we are expecting the next phase to come hot on its heels."

"StoneHaven is the obvious location to keep everyone appeased," Lukas says. "Have they looked into where they're going to establish the mint?"

"Why not the old mint?" Dune suggests. "I went there a few times with a girl I was dating—"

"—and when you say dating you mean sexing at regular intervals, right?"

Dune shrugs. "Isn't that what dating is?"

We all shake our heads.

I laugh and take the lead on this. "Not at all, but back to the point of the story. How does this tie into the old mint?"

"Right. So, the girl I wasn't dating but was sexing at regular intervals worked as a curator at the Central Mint Museum. We spent many incredible nights exploring the place after close and giving one another private tours if you know what I mean."

I nod. "We all know what you mean."

"One thing that stuck with me was her going on about almost all of the original working mint machinery surviving the Wars of Power. That's why it made such a good museum. The presses and the smelting heaters and all the equipment survived."

"That sounds promising." I finish tying my laces and sit up. "Maybe we could talk to this girl and get some more information. What's her name?"

Dunes sandy blond brow arches. "That was like three years ago. Besides, I don't think I ever knew her name. I always called her mint girl."

"Mint girl?" Tundra repeats. "When you made plans to get together you didn't even call her by name?"

"Don't get huffy with me. I must've known her name at some point at the beginning but when it got a little fuzzy I called her mint girl. She thought it was a cute little pet name."

"And she never realized you didn't know her real name?" Lukas asks, his eyes wide.

Dune shrugs. "Maybe she did. Maybe it didn't matter. The sex was great and neither one of us was looking to settle down, so what does it matter?"

I wave the question away and move on. Dune is a unique kind of man. "Let's look into the Central Mint Museum as a potential site for the realm mint establishment. If it's in good condition, we could be up and running quickly if needed. What else did I miss?"

Lukas finishes sending a message on his tablet and slides it into his pants pocket. "We still need to find Breard's cache of weapons and where the black-market portal gate has been established. Until that's closed, it doesn't matter if we confiscate the illegal weapons or not, he'll keep bringing more into the realm."

I slide deeper in my seat and flop back against the cushion. "There has to be a way to detect where a portal to another realm has been opened. How did you guys find the spot for the Pennsylvania portal after Hawk's father destroyed the established Portal Gate in Kansas?"

"Calli did that," Lukas says. "She sensed the magic of portal openings or where a rift could be made for one. The Quint traveled across the United States with a map of the ancient locations long forgotten and she flew in her phoenix form to gauge the potential of opening a rift there."

"We certainly can't ask that of her now," I say, deflated. "She just had a baby two days ago."

Lukas seems to agree. "And there's no guarantee she would be able to sense it anyway. While they searched back then, finding and establishing a portal gate was her destiny as the Fae Phoenix. She may no longer have the ability. She has completed her destiny."

"If I might offer an opinion," Shadow says, holding up a

finger. "Admittedly, I don't know Calli as well as you and Honor do, but I know her well enough to say for certain you should at least pose the question and allow her the chance to weigh in. If she feels she is well enough to help in the search, isn't it her answer to give?"

Maybe but I don't like it.

I sigh. "I'm not a fan of putting Calli in that position. Given any task like this, she's going to dive headfirst into it. She has a baby to consider now. It's not fair of us to put her in danger."

"So, what of Jaxx, Hawk, Kotah, and Brant?" Tundra asks. "They also have a baby to consider now. Does having a child mean a person is no longer capable of taking on risks? Will the five of them be removed from our list of backup forces simply because there is a child?"

"Well, no."

"Then what does Calli giving birth have to do with her being a viable answer to a problem?"

I chuckle. "Why do I feel like you're a more enlightened feminist than I am, Tundra?"

"I don't know what that is."

I wave that away. "You're right. Considering Calli ineligible to go out on a mission because she gave birth is archaic and absurd. My bad."

"And isn't she invincible as a phoenix?" Dune asks, scanning our faces looking confused. "She *is*, right? She's bulletproof, fire-resistant, and her healing powers are unmatched. What danger would she be in while flying through the sky?"

Well, when he puts it that way...

"Fine, I'll ask her but as Lukas said, she may no longer have that ability now that her destiny is fulfilled."

"It can't hurt to ask is all I'm saying," Dune says, his attention shifting to focus on Shadow. "You've got a bit of a nosebleed there, Counselor. You might want to get it before it drips on your shirt."

Lukas is quick with a box of tissues and comes to the rescue. "What's this about? Do you get nosebleeds often?"

"No. Never." Shadow leans forward pressing the cloth to his face. "I've had a bit of a headache... it's probably just the stress of the past week."

Moonshade stands on her hind legs, pawing for Shadow to pick her up. I shuffle over, scoop her up, and shift the wolf cub to sit on my lap so she can see him while Lukas tends to the problem at hand.

"Pinch the bridge of your nose," Dune says, raising his hand and gesturing in mid-air. "Trust me, I've had a million nose-bleeds, and that works best."

Tundra chuckles. "A million natural nosebleeds? Or a million gushers from being punched in the face?"

Dune scowls. "Is that relevant to this situation? The point here is stopping it not determining how it started."

"He's right," I say, chuckling. "Getting it stopped is the important thing."

The sensation of Lukas's magic building in the air shifts my focus from Shadow to our in-house mage. Lukas's lips are moving in silent spellcasting and the worried look on his face tells me it's not as easy to stop as he thinks it should be.

Still, in the end, he steps back and exhales. "Better?"

Shadow turns the cloth and wipes. "You tell me. I'm blind, remember?"

"It's better," Tundra says. "Crisis averted."

The two of them laugh but I'm looking at Lukas. I see the truth in his eyes—the crisis *isn't* averted.

By his shadowed expression, I'd say the crisis is just beginning.

Lukas

The five of us head back to the castle and take the new four-seater side-by-side ATVs I imported. Hawk and I discussed the terrain and the need for speed during emergencies and thought these were the answer to the problem of us traveling back and forth to the castle on the quick.

Tundra is driving Shadow and Dune in the buggy ahead of Honor and me, and Moonshade is racing along beside us with her tongue hanging out and her tail wagging like mad.

Elves and wildlings have heightened hearing, so I asked Tundra to take a lead and put some distance between us so I can speak to Honor without Shadow hearing what's being said.

"That nosebleed wasn't just a nosebleed, was it?"

I shake my head and meet Honor's worried gaze. "I don't think so, no. I should've been able to stop a simple nosebleed without effort. That wasn't simple."

Honor grips the hair flying wild and loose by her face and stops it from whipping around. "I sensed something off with his mental energy when we first sat down to eat this afternoon. I'm worried it's something to do with his Oracle powers activating and him not having the proper training to know how to shield his mind."

Fuck. "I thought we'd have more time before that took hold. I sent out a few feelers in the other realm to see if anyone is willing to help us but with everything that happened this week, I haven't had a chance to go to the other realm and follow up."

We bump over a thick root, and Honor grips the roll bar. Man, these things have balls. My lunch churns in my gut and it has nothing to do with the ride and everything to do with Shadow's situation.

"You think you have to go to the other realm?"

I meet Honor's gaze and nod. "Unless you have contacts within the oracle community in this realm, I do."

"Sorry. I don't. Oracles are a secretive sect and hostile toward intruders. I guess we go with your contacts. First, we'll check on Calli, then we see to the Amberloq, then we'll consider a trip to the other realm so you can meet with your contacts about Shadow."

I hate that securing Shadow's mental state is third on the list but when I consider it objectively, the first two things on the list could be done in a couple of hours.

"Agreed. Let's getter done."

We slow down before we break from the trees and by the time we pull around the north end of the castle to approach the King's Tower, we're going at a perfectly respectable pace.

Well, the buggy is... my heart rate isn't.

Honor casts a sideways glance at me and leans close. "Are you all right?"

"I'm not normally an alarmist but is there a tank parked on my chest. It sure feels like it."

She reaches over and squeezes my hand. "Shadow's situation scares me too."

"I'm not accustomed to being scared. I'm the guy that makes sure nothing bad happens."

"You'll do that again for Shadow. We both will."

I hope so. "Somewhere along the path of getting mated I became emotionally invested. That's new for me. I wouldn't say I spent my life being detached, but other than Hawk, no one's life ever mattered as much or more than my own. That has changed."

She squeezes my hand again and smiles at the other three hopping out of the other buggy. "I know exactly how you feel. So, let's do what we need to do so we can give it our full attention."

I pull the keys from the ignition and nod. "Divide and conquer."

∾

Tundra

While Honor and Shadow go to the King's Tower to look at the young phoenix, Lukas, Dune, and I, navigate the corridors of the castle and meet up with Rhylan in the security room in the lower level.

When we arrive, Rhylan looks up, surprise clear on his face. "Hey, I didn't know you guys were coming. I was about to leave and go back to the suite for dinner. We're still on for dinner, aren't we?"

Lukas nods. "We are. Honor is looking forward to time with Calli. While they catch up, we thought we'd make ourselves useful and check in on the progress of the realm currency. Dune had an idea about where we could set up shop in a pinch if we needed to."

Rhylan turns his attention to Dune and for him to join the conversation. "By all means, let's hear it. What's on your mind?"

Dune goes on to tell Rhy about the Central Mint Museum and I have to admit, he is both tactical in his assessment of the location and professional in his delivery of the information. It's been a long time in coming, but I always knew he had it in him. It sounds pretentious to say I'm proud of him for manning up, but I am.

"The old mint is actually on our list of locations to consider." Rhylan turns to the war table and picks up his tablet. With a couple of swipes on the screen, he brings up a list of locations, each with an image beside it in the right margin.

"Yeah, that's it." Dune points to the fourth building down the list. "Who's doing site inspections and narrowing down the list?"

"Hawk and Creed planned to do that together but with Calli and what happened, none of her mates have strayed far."

"And it will probably be a long while before they do," Lukas says. "I've never seen Hawk so rattled about anything in all the years we've been working and hanging out together."

Rhylan nods. "I think it'll be a long time before any of the mates get past Calli dying like that."

"Dying?" Dune says. "I heard it was bad but—"

"Really bad," Lukas says. "From what Doc told me, the baby couldn't be born by natural methods, and every attempt to take him out by surgical measures failed because of Calli's healing and her body's instinct to protect the child. At the end, when the little guy was ready to be born, he ignited into flame and burned his way out from the inside."

"That's horrific," Dune says, his expression twisted.

"It was," Rhylan says. "Calli didn't survive and for a full six minutes, Hawk, Jaxx, Kotah, and Brant thought they'd lost her."

"But then she resurrected," I guess.

Lukas nods. "It has been a running question since the beginning. Was her phoenix rebirth a one-time thing or part of her abilities? We were lucky enough that when we found out the answer, it held a happy result."

"Holy hell." Dune scrubs his fingers through his hair. "I had no idea."

Lukas frowns. "It's not something they want to talk about. They're not over it and likely never will be."

The room falls quiet for a long moment and then Lukas points to the list of potential currency locations. "Back to establishing a mint. How far down the list have you gotten?"

Rhylan taps his tablet and a large red X appears on the first and second listings. "The first one doesn't have the capacity for the power needed to run a mint. It's in the center of an area running on the old grid system. It would take more time to update the grid and get things working than it would to build a new mint in a better part of the quadrant."

"And the second?"

"It's owned by a shell corporation that ties back to one of the one-percenters listed as a supporter of Laryssa and Ruic Breard."

"So that's a hell no," Lukas says.

"Exactly. It has to be a realm-owned building for this to work. If there are private interests involved, it opens the door for corruption all over again."

I agree. "Can we be any help in working through the list? Dune and I can cover a great deal of ground quite quickly. If you tell us the parameters of what you need to know, we are happy to be put to use."

"Creed is already working on that," Rhylan says. "He put together a team inviting a liaison from each of the quadrants and they're set to start in the morning. I need you guys working on finding the rebel gate and shutting down their access to illegal weapons."

"We have an idea about that," Lukas says. "Honor is probably speaking with Calli about that as we speak."

"Good, then let's head back to the tower and see where we are on ending this bullshit."

CHAPTER FIFTEEN

Honor

"Welcome, welcome," Creed says, opening the door when Shadow and I arrive at the royal residence. "Glad you finally decided to open your eyes and face the world, Sleeping Beauty. I wish *I* could laze about and sleep for three days. Alas, I don't have that luxury."

I roll my eyes at my brother and continue inside. "They should've woken me up. I assure you if given the choice I wouldn't have missed the birth of my nephew."

Creed's expression tightens and he leans close. "It's better you missed it. It wasn't a good time and they're all trying to put it behind them. Don't mention it around the guys at all. They can't take it."

"I heard. Lukas told me what happened at lunch. Trust me, I don't want to think about it any more than they do. He assured me she's all right now though, right?"

"Come inside and see for yourself."

Creed leads us toward the Great Room and Kotah and Brant come out to greet us.

"Honor. We're so pleased you're feeling better," Kotah says. "Calli's been worried."

She's been worried about me? "I heard she and I have some catching up to do. I also heard there's a baby I need to be introduced to."

"You heard correctly," Kotah says. "Ashborn Benjamin Jonathan Northwood Barron."

I laugh. "Wow, that's a mouthful."

Kotah shrugs. "It'll be Ash Barron for every day, but we all got to add a pick. Benjamin is Brant's foster father's name. Jonathan is Jaxx's father. Northwood in case anything happens to me, and he needs to assume my place as Fae Prime until the Northwood term of reign ends. And, of course, Barron because we took Hawk's name when we mated."

"That's a lot of meaning behind one little guy's name."

"It is, but he's going to be one amazing wildling boy. He's already famous simply for being born. He needed a name befitting his importance."

"Well, with the five of you as parents, I have no doubt he'll make both realms proud."

Brant grins. "You bet your fine ass he will."

Creed chuckles and squeezes my shoulder. "I'd say they're getting carried away as proud papas but the kid is truly special."

Brant chuffs. "Special? That's it? You forgot beautiful, smart, and perfect."

"And has all five of you wrapped around his little finger, I bet," I add.

Kotah breaks out into a wide grin. "Oh, that goes without saying. Come. Calli is anxious to see you."

The welcoming committee leads us into the Great Room. Jaxx is sitting on one of the couches holding the sleeping baby on his lap. Hawk is fawning over the swathed bundle taking pictures with his tablet. And Kotah and Brant jog back over to check if they missed anything by stepping away.

"Hey, girlfriend."

Calli jumps up from the couch and hustles over to hug me. She looks healthy and whole and I'm relieved because even though Lukas told me as much, seeing is believing. "I'm glad you're here."

"Nothing like being late for the party. I'm so sorry." I squeeze her hands in mine and send her a heartfelt look of apology. She died and I wasn't there.

Sure, I was doing my duty as the Guardian of the Crown, but still... I have a duty to my bestie too.

Calli waves my apology away. "There was nothing you could've done. Now we're solidly focusing on the little spark plug being here."

"Don't call him spark plug." Hawk scowls. "You know I hate that."

Calli laughs. "You called me spitfire. Why can't I call him spark plug?"

Hawk gives her a droll stare and then goes back to being a shutterbug.

Hilarious.

"I must say, you look great. I don't know what I was expecting, but you bouncing off the couch looking as spry as ever wasn't it."

She shrugs, her blonde ponytail waving behind her. "The beauty of magical phoenix healing. I'm blessed."

I tilt my head toward her mates doting over their newborn child. "You are."

"I'm also heavily outnumbered. I was looking forward to a little estrogen balancing in the household. Now I've added more wildling testosterone instead."

"About that... how is he a *he*? What happened to phoenix babies always coming out girls? How did baby Liza end up being Ashborn?"

Calli laughs. "Don't ask me. Of all the people here, I know

the least about being a wildling or a phoenix. I just go by what everyone else says, but in this case, everyone got it wrong."

"Calli breaks all the rules," Jaxx says, barely able to lift his gaze from the swaddled bundle laying in the seam of his two legs. His socked feet are on the coffee table and with his knees up, he's created an incline for the wee boy to snuggle into. "If something is expected of her, she's bound to do the exact opposite."

"True story," Brant says.

"She's not one for convention," Kotah says.

Hawk stops taking pictures long enough to look up and wink at his mate. "She keeps things interesting, that's for sure."

Calli waves away their words and tugs me over to see the little man.

"Oh, he is a cutie."

Calli grins. "I know, right? And it's not even us being biased or polite. He's a really good-looking kid."

"He's got a strong gene pool to draw from," I say, tilting my head toward her guys. "His daddies are hotties, one and all."

Shadow looks over at me and laughs. "You've got four hotties of your own. You don't need to be building up their egos."

I step back from looking at the baby and grin. "It's called window shopping. A girl can admire the beauty of things without needing to take it home."

"Does that go both ways, Princess?" he asks. "Do we men get to go window shopping?"

"No," Calli and I both say together.

The two of us laugh and leave the boys to their conversations. Because wildling hearing is so acute, I avoid the topic of what she's been up to the past few days altogether. This is a celebration, not a post-mortem.

Calli gives me an extremely abbreviated version of the shock of the baby being born a boy, and then points over at the four of them and shakes her head. "They're crazy—obsessed. I worried it would be bad when they were talking non-stop about their baby girl. I think this might be worse."

A timer sounds somewhere and Jaxx sits up straighter and lifts the baby boy for a handoff. "Oh, no. We would've been the same if he'd been born a girl as expected. The only real shame is that Mama's been knitting pink things for months. Now she's going to feel like she has nothing ready for baby Ash."

"I'm sorry about that," Calli says. "And for all the wasted money Hawk spent on the nursery."

"Nonsense," Hawk says, rushing around the arm of the couch to accept the baby handoff. "I had the designers of the new house pack up the pink to put it in storage for some lucky baby girl. Ash's room was redone and is ready for us to take him home."

"So, you're going back? Like... right away?"

Calli meets my gaze and shrugs. "We were waiting to see you first, but yeah, that's the plan. Kotah is needed in the other realm. As much as the citizens have been patient with us being here, a king needs to spend time in his kingdom."

"Yeah, of course. I get that."

Calli's gaze narrows. "Why? Do you need something? You look like you need something."

"Actually, I need a favor. I don't suppose you're feeling up to flying phoenix over the quadrant before you go, are you? We need to find the portal gate the rebels are using so we can shut down the inflow of illegal weapons. Lukas mentioned you had a sensitivity to the energy and could detect it."

"I could, yeah," Calli says. "I'm not sure I still do but I'm willing to try."

Cue four wildling males becoming hyper-focused on our conversation.

"Are you certain you feel up to shifting forms and flying, *Chigua*?" Kotah asks.

"Absolutely. After we eat, I'll feed Ash and be good to go work off my dinner. I should be able to tell if I'm still a rift detector by flying over the Dornte Portal Hub. If I sense it, we'll go after the rebel gate."

"I'm not sure I like this idea," Hawk says.

His concern seems to be shared by Jaxx, Brant, and Kotah, too. Calli offers the four of them a patient smile. "I love you all. Thank you for worrying about me but I'm fully healed and excited to take an hour or two for myself to do something important. This matters."

"No one is suggestin' it doesn't, Kitten, but what if you're not ready? What if Ash needs you?"

"He has the four of you."

"Three," Hawk says. "Since this is a flying task, I'll go with you. Honor, Tundra, and Dune can come too, but you're not going anywhere without one of us."

Calli frowns. "I will forgive the dictator caveman routine in light of recent events. That's fine. You can fly with me, but I promise you all, I'm one-hundy percent ready to get out and about."

The men lock gazes and seem to be having a private conversation on their mental communication channel. A moment later, Jaxx's growl rumbles in the air. "You win again, Kitten. Hawk will escort you with Dune, Tundra, and whoever else goes. Brant, Kotah, and I will stay back with Ash and pack to go home when you're done."

"You're assuming I'll find it my first time out?" Calli asks. "I'm good, but I'm not sure I'm that good."

"First try or tenth doesn't matter. Trying is all I'm asking. Now, sorry Hawk, but if we're going out after dinner, I'm playing the bestie card and take my turn holding this bundle of sleeping bliss while I can. You can have him back when he's screaming or stinking."

Hawk arches an imperious brow. "So, I give him to you content and clean and you return him dirty and disgruntled?"

"Yep. That's how Auntie Honor rolls."

~

Dune

Dinner with Honor's family is fun but through the entire event, my mind is filtering through the details of finding the portal gate, resettling the Amberloq refugees, and wondering about Ruic Breard's plans, Shadow's health, and how we're going to reestablish an Amberloq force going forward.

"You've been quiet tonight." Tundra is standing next to me with a bottle of ale in his hand. "Why are you out here?"

The rest of the group is lapping up the social scene in the Great Room, but I stepped outside to get some air on the balcony.

"Is everything all right?" he asks.

I glance up at the first moon burning bright against the night sky and breathe deeply. "Everything is fine. My mind is just racing with ideas and details and a million things to consider if we're going to come out of this goblin rebellion on top."

"Finding the unsanctioned gate will help."

"It will, but there's still so much to be done."

He offers me his drink and I take a long swallow. When I hand it back to him, he captures my wrist and closes the distance between us. Claiming my mouth, he slides his free hand behind my back and pulls me close.

The contact is aggressive and unexpected but welcome. Tundra is always welcome.

His tongue sweeps into my mouth and he runs an indecent caress over the sensitive flesh at the base of my wings. The nerve endings send a heated zing of sensation straight to my cock.

I curse as my body responds in an instant.

"What are you doing?" I hiss, the front of my pants growing tighter.

Instead of answering, he uses his hold on my wrist and pulls me into the shadows. A racing heartbeat later, my pants are around my thighs and his lips are parting over the engorged tip of my throbbing cock.

"Slecking hell, what are you doing?"

I grip the sides of his head to push him away but I haven't got the willpower. Instead, I release my hips and give in to the hot suction of his mouth.

The voices of Honor's family inside are muffled but not so far away that they couldn't come out here at any moment and find the two of us. Part of me wants to care about that. A much bigger part of me doesn't give a shit.

Up and down, Tundra rides the length of my solid erection from root to tip. The alternation between the heat of his mouth and the cool breeze that hits on each retreat is amazing. And then there's the way his teeth gently score my heated flesh.

Closing my eyes, I tip my head back and let the sensations take hold. Tundra is thorough in all things. He's gifted with his attention to detail and he's in tune with the people around him.

All great things from the person sucking on your cock. We spend a few more heated moments in the shadows before my mind kicks in. As incredible as this is, we're still on the balcony of the King's Tower and are about to go out flying with the Fae Phoenix and her mate. Now is not the time to drag things out.

The pressure of my release is building hard and fast.

My hips rock, thrusting into his mouth as the burn in my sac takes hold and my need to orgasm ignites.

Slecking hell, it feels so good.

My breathing hitches and I let it take hold.

My hips lock.

My orgasm breaks free.

My world shatters.

When my breathing settles and Tundra straightens in front of me, he's wearing a smug smile.

"What was that for?"

"You didn't like it? It seemed like you did."

I bark a laugh and do up my pants. "I definitely liked it. I'm just not sure what inspired it."

Tundra grins. "We didn't get much time together today and I wanted to show you I'm proud of you."

"Do you give everyone you're proud of a blowjob?"

He laughs. "No. Only you."

I let that sink in. "Thank you, by the way. It was unexpected but great."

Tundra tilts his head toward the door back inside. "I volunteered to come to get you. We're almost ready to leave. Calli had to finish feeding the baby. She should be done now."

I follow him back inside where Lukas is standing inside the door. When he sees us, he flashes me a knowing smile and raises a fist to knuckle bump Tundra.

"What? Are you the bouncer working the door?"

Lukas grins. "I may not have feathers, but I make a damned good wingman. Just ensuring a little privacy."

I raise my knuckles and he smiles, obliging me with a bump. "Thanks."

CHAPTER SIXTEEN

Honor

$\mathcal{I}$ 've only seen Calli's phoenix form once before, and that wasn't even while she was flying. The day Dune and Tundra made their entrance into my life, she flamed out in her woman on fire form during a fight in my suite.

Being in the air with her, flying with her, feeling the incredible heat she radiates while in this form—it's incredible.

She is incredible.

She's come so far from the scared and angry runaway I met when I time-shifted to find her. Time-shifting isn't an easy or a common thing. If it wasn't for Brizbin helping me the first few times with the traveler's bed, there's no way I could have done it.

But between my natural gifts as a mind guardian, Brizbin helping me with the traveler's bed when I escaped Laryssa's captivity, and the prophetic knowledge that one day a spunky street rat from the Human Realm would be the mythical savior to unite our two realms, countless lives were changed.

The hardest part was finding a human host in the right area

in the final moments of life so I could assume her identity. Riley Taggert was the unwitting savior of our quadrant. I wish I could've thanked her in some way.

The only solace is knowing that instead of dying as a drug overdosed runaway that no one ever mourned, her death held meaning. She was the unknown soldier of our war against corruption and greed.

"Is everything all right?" Creed asks, his long, silver hair blowing in the wind as we fly.

"Sorry. Just thinking about how far Calli's come and what it took to get here."

"She's incredible." Creed spins in the air beside me, gesturing to the flaming bird. "The first time I saw her, she kicked Vikarus and Rhylan's asses."

Rhy's dragon lets off a hiss beside us and Creed laughs. "Don't be testy. It's true. She took on both of you and shut you down hard."

The dragon grunts but there's no real heat in it.

Pride swells in my chest. "That's my girl."

He grins. "You did a great job preparing her for what was to come. Our freedom is because of you. Reclaiming our lives and our quadrant is all your doing. I doubt any other Guardian of the Crown has gone to such lengths to protect the people of not only our quadrant but the entire realm."

I don't know if I'd go that far, but having my big brother's approval is nice. "How much haze were you drinking tonight?"

He chuckles, fluttering his wings and holding out his arms to catch the night breeze. "I can't believe it's been so long since the two of us flew together. Do you remember how wild we were in the air as kids?"

I laugh, holding my arms out to the side like him and spinning in a corkscrew as my hair catches in the wind. "I do. Somewhere along the line growing up stole something from us."

"Well, it's time we steal it back. From now on, we're going to take the time to remember who we are and what's important to us. Moments like this need to become part of our life again."

"Agreed."

Calli shifts course in the air and circles over the Dornte Portal Hub. With a shrill screech, she lifts the tip of one of her wings and gives us what loosely translates into a thumb's up.

"Excellent. She can still sense portal magic," I say.

Tundra swoops over to join our flight path. "There's a great deal more portal energy in our realm than there was in hers. Do you think that will complicate her search for the illegal gate?"

"It might." I flutter my wings and shift to face him. "It'll depend if she's sensing portal magic or rift magic. When she searched for the potential sites to establish the portal between worlds, it was the power of rift energy she sensed. If that's still the case, she'll be fine."

"Then let's hope that's the case," Creed says.

I love watching my brother soar through the night sky. It's amazing to see him so happy. Between his mating and assuming the realm and now reclaiming a bit of his former self, he's the man I always knew he could be.

Calli lets off another squawk and veers right, picking up speed. Hawk is flying tight to her side. His wildling bird is a speck of a silhouette next to her brilliance. "It's incredible he can be that close to her. She's frying my eyebrows and we're nowhere near as close."

Creed laughs. "It's a mating thing. They're the only ones who can touch her and be near her when she's on fire or even after."

The power of mating...

I glance over at Dune and Tundra. Our union bonding is taking hold and I couldn't be happier with the progress we're making as a unit. The sex this afternoon highlighted just how far we've come.

The first time we were together, Shadow wasn't part of our group and it was solely about the pleasure of sex. Today, it was about deepening the relationships between the five members of our quint.

To me, that's progress.

Dune is finally in sync with the group and if things continue to improve with him, I don't see why the five of us can't be as close and in love as Calli and her mates.

Hope flutters in my chest.

I never imagined I'd want this to work out as much as I do. I've always known there was a possibility I'd bond with the Biome Generals but I didn't expect it to bloom into true and deep emotion.

It's nice when life surprises you.

Calli slows her flight and tilts her wing to drop into a wide arc. The six of us follow. Below us there is nothing but farmland... or at least that's how it seems. Maybe it's an underground facility or a powerful glamor or they've hidden things with some other form of magic.

It certainly isn't somewhere we would have pegged as a location for the unsanctioned portal gate.

She circles a bit more and then squawks twice. That's the signal for finding the energy signature.

She did it!

Tundra and I both reach for our watches at the same time. I click the coordinates tracker and ensure it locks on our location. Without stopping, Calli arcs back the way we came and we follow her once again.

She promised her mates this was an intel-gathering mission only and it is. We found the location and Ruic Breard and his asshole rebels are none the wiser. Those goblins have no idea they've been busted—

Rhylan lets off a fierce growl and banks left, pumping his wings with a fury that doesn't bode well.

Creed curses and follows.

That takes Dune, Tundra, and I off the plan as well. Our

primary duty is to protect the king. If he's flying off, we've got no choice but to follow.

Our return home is officially sidetracked as Calli and Hawk join the chaos.

"What's he doing?" I shout, pushing to catch up to Creed. "What's wrong?"

A second dragon comes out of the night and collides with Rhylan in flight. The two of them are identical. They collide with a crashing force and grapple at each other with dagger-sharp claws.

The sight takes my breath. They are massive, powerful, and fighting one another with a ferocity that negates them being twin brothers.

I'm not sure what to do and am about to consult with Dune and Tundra when Calli blows a steaming stream of fire at one of the dragons and knocks him tumbling backward.

My heart is racing as she follows through with her attack. She flies straight at the scaled beast and takes him to the ground. The air echoes with a thundering rumble and when the dust clears, we can see why.

A massive culvert has been left in the ground.

Calli drove him into the ground with such force and speed they made a rut in the earth. The fighting foes wrestle against one another.

Fire roars and claws slash.

The second dragon drops to the rim of the culvert. Standing at his full height, it comes to his shoulders. When he shifts back, I'm relieved to see it's Rhylan.

"How did she pick which one was Vik?" Creed asks looking furious. "Without our ability to speak over a mental connection, I would've been lost myself."

"Calli has always been incredible at the shell game. If she watched the original collision, she would've picked out which one was Rhy and which one was Vik."

Rhylan climbs out and Creed lands beside him.

Rhylan scowls and moves to stand in front of Creed. "What the hell are you doing? Right now, you're not my mate. You're the King of Dornte and we're about to have a confrontation with a known rebel conspirator. You can't put yourself in these kinds of situations."

Hawk shifts as he lands beside us looking pissed. "My question is, how is he here? We arrested him, interrogated him, and had him locked in a holding cell."

Rhylan shrugs. "No idea. He did play a big part in building the security facility and its protocols. Maybe he made himself a back door escape. Or maybe he still has friends on the inside. The answer means less than what's happening here."

"What *is* happening here?" Calli asks. She climbs out of the rut and thankfully, was able to flash her clothes back on this time. "Rhy, I caught your brother for you. I gotta say, that workout went a long way at working off some of my pent-up stresses about the birthing."

I chuckle. "You have always liked to pick a fight when you were stressed."

Calli grins. "True story."

"How the slecking hell did you get free?" Rhylan snaps, ignoring us. "And why the hell would you run right back here to report in with Ruic Breard's asshole rebels? Do you want a slecking goblin in charge of the realm over Creed?"

Vikarus shifts back to his human form and curses. "I know all the ins and outs of Thornebane security, remember? Getting free was about nothing more than biding my time and waiting for my opportunity. As for the goblin thing, of course, I don't want goblins in charge. I'm not the idiot you think I am."

"Then why were you at the sex club with him the night you shot Lukas. And why did you race back here the moment you escaped custody?"

"What are my other options?"

"How about *not* siding with assholes bent on destroying me and my mates? How about remembering we're brothers and not just brothers but twins? Where the fuck is your loyalty?"

"Where's yours?" he snaps. "This whole mess started when you crossed the line with Creed and switched sides. Where was your loyalty then?"

"It was with the realm and the rightful heir of the quadrant. You never liked Laryssa or the Blood Witch, so don't pretend you did. You willingly chose sides and now you're too stubborn to admit you were wrong."

"Because it's too late to fix any of it. Eyes on the horizon, right? What's done is done. You made your choices and I made mine."

"But I chose for love, and you chose for money and power."

Vik barks a laugh. "Says the mated prince of the realm. You realize how ridiculous that statement is, right? You're living in the slecking castle running security for the king of the realm. It sounds like you're doing well in the money and power department."

"Let's wrap this up, folks," Hawk says frowning. "The point of the evening was a scouting mission. If we allow the evil twin to have his way, he'll no doubt notify Breard we're on to him. We can't let that happen."

"What are you suggesting, babe?" Calli asks.

Hawk points to light in the sky at the same moment the rhythmic hum of helicopter rotors sounds above us. "You're under arrest—again—Vik."

Vik doesn't seem to appreciate Hawk's take on that.

Creed holds up a hand. "Vik, enough. Don't fight and don't fuss. Just come with us and once this goblin rebellion is crushed, we'll sit down and figure out a different path for you. I know you were angry about Rhy and me. You reacted badly but nothing's been done that can't be undone with a little time."

"Except him shooting and almost killing Lukas," I snap. "That can't be undone."

"You're right. It can't," Creed says, "but thankfully he didn't die. My point is that I'd rather this conflict between brothers ends sooner rather than later. It's time to heal and rebuild."

I'm not keen on forgiving Vik for his sins. Yes, I've grown to respect Rhylan and even care about him and his relationship with my brother but he chose Creed when it came down to it.

Vikarus didn't.

The helicopter lands fifty feet to my right and I leave them to figure it out. Creed's the king, not me.

I point toward the chopper and excuse myself. "I'm going to say hi to the pilot. Figure out what the plan is and let's get going as soon as possible. We may not be on top of Ruic's hideaway, but we're not far off. We're still hoping for the element of surprise, aren't we?"

"Yeah, we are," Rhylan says. "Vik, for once, don't dig in. Come with us and let us take down Breard without you being involved. We're going to crush him. We know it and you do too. Choose the right side this time. Choose love."

Vikarus looks at his twin and his face screws up. "Is this what mating has done to you? You're a sap."

Rhylan rolls his eyes and shrugs. "It might sound that way, but we both know that before Calli broke up our fight and threw you into the earth, I was beating the snot out of you."

Vik snorts. "You wish. You're the brains. I'm the brawn. You can't fight nature."

A sad smile settles on Rhylan's face and he offers him a hand to help him out of the culverted dirt. "You're right. You can't fight nature so stop fighting me. We're part of one another and like you said, I'm the brains. Trust me when I say you need to course correct. It's not too late for us to salvage our relationship but that window is closing fast."

As much as I don't like Vik, I'm a sucker for a happy ending and I know how close the dragon twins used to be. It would be nice for Rhylan if they could find that again... as long as it isn't near me.

There is a long pause while the two stare at one another and I assume Vik is running through his options in his mind. Eventually, he curses and accepts the hand offered to him. "I'm not your prisoner. I won't be kept in a cell like a criminal. If you try, I'll just escape again."

Rhy dips his chin. "Fine. You're not a prisoner. You will be sequestered though. You've fucked us over too many times for you to get a pass."

"You say fucked over. I say survived to fight another day."

"Uh-huh... and like Creed said, when the goblin rebellion is crushed, we'll revisit your skills and find you a new path that doesn't put us at odds."

Vik rolls his eyes. "Fine, but if I don't like the path you pick, I'm not doing it. My days of blindly following your lead are over."

Rhy clasps wrists with him and hauls him out of the hole. "How about we worry about today first. Tomorrow's problems can wait."

CHAPTER SEVENTEEN

Lukas

$\mathscr{A}$n hour after Hawk sent me the text to fire up the helicopter to come pick up Vikarus, we're back at Thornebane Castle having a sit down with Rhylan's twin brother. The guy says he's had a change of heart and since he's no longer on Ruic Breard's payroll, he'll give us the down and dirty on the underground facility Calli found.

"No offense, Dragon," Dune says, "but we can't trust anything your twin has to say. He's fought against us. He's infiltrated us. He's lied to us. And now, all of a sudden, he's turning his life around to be brothers again? I don't buy it."

Rhylan nods. "I understand the apprehension—seriously, I do. I know Vik better than anyone in the two realms. Yes, he's a dick and he's headstrong—"

"—I can hear you, asshole."

"Nothing I wouldn't and haven't said to your face, asshole," Rhylan snaps back. "But my point is, I believe him. If he gives us intel on the underground facility, it's more of a heads-up than if he doesn't. We don't have time to research the bunker to find the portal rift and plan everything out. It's between going in blind and going in with possibly useful intel. If it's wrong, we're no worse off. We can consider it unreliable information until we verify it ourselves."

I don't love the idea but he's not wrong.

Having any idea of what we're facing down there is better than nothing. "Okay, give him a grid on the war table and map us a layout with as many details as possible. We won't know until we're in the heat of things if he's being straight with us, but it's an acceptable risk."

"Says you," Hawk snaps. "Calli wants to be part of finding and shutting down the rift. When she's involved there is no such thing as an acceptable risk."

"I understand, but as Dune said earlier, Calli is the most indestructible of any of us. In any of her flaming forms, she's bulletproof, she can fly, and no one can get close enough to harm her."

Hawk flashes me a heated scowl but nothing he does intimidates me anymore.

"Happy wife, happy life, my friend. She wants to see this through and it's empowering for her to be in control of things. Kotah, Keyla, Shadow, and Creed will stay with Ash. That leaves you, Brant, and Jaxx to come with us to back her up."

"Not that she needs backup," Honor says, her brow creasing. "Having a baby didn't change who she is today from who she was last week or last month. She's the same tough, feisty female she's always been and she needs the four of you to understand that and believe in her as an equal."

"Thanks, girlfriend," Calli says, stepping through the door and joining us in the security room. "I couldn't have said it better myself. So, when do we leave?"

175

Tundra

"For this incursion, we have a three-tiered objective," Honor says, addressing the group. "Lukas will go with Calli and the Quint to find the rift and shut down the gate. She can sense the magic and should be able to hone in and lead them straight there."

"Yeah, baby," Calli says, taking a little curtsy. "It's an honor to be nominated but it'll be even better when I burn their bootleg access to our realm to the ground."

Dune lifts his hand, looking serious. "Can we keep the blazing fires to a minimum until we're finished and are sure we can get out of the bunker? Burning alive underground isn't on my list. Not all of us are flameproof."

"An excellent point," Lukas says, "and considering we'll be at our most vulnerable during the bottleneck of getting in and out of this place, adding a raging fire eating up our oxygen would be bad."

Calli nods. "I'll keep that in mind."

"All right," Honor continues. "The Phoenix Quint is tasked with destroying the gate to the Human Realm while the rest of us are working on the gun cache and taking out Ruic and his goblin troops."

"My twin says there are usually about twenty guys down there, but unfortunately Ruic isn't one of them."

"He's too much of a coward to get into the trenches with his men," Hawk says, disdain heavy in his tone. "He thinks himself a puppet master."

"He can think that all he wants," Honor says, doing a final weapon check before holstering her sidearm. "We go after him next."

"First the rift and the guns," Lukas says, addressing the FCO teams accompanying us. "Alpha Squad you're on breach and secure. Beta Squad, you clean up their mess and ensure anyone they mow down are gift-wrapped and brought out of the bunker so we can blow the entire place in a hurry if we have to."

"Roger that," Connor MacDougall says. "We'll tag 'em and they'll bag 'em. Right boys?"

A round of nods tells us that everyone is clear on the objectives.

"According to my traitorous brother, there's only one access point. He says they've got eyes on the entrance but no lockdown or security features in place. Take that for what it's worth."

"Which isn't much," Lukas says, frowning. "Sorry, Rhy, but for the safety of our men, we've got to consider your brother as a big, fat liar."

Rhylan waves off the apology. "No offense taken. I don't know if we can trust him either. So, yeah, take all precautions necessary."

"You heard the man," Honor says, raising a cupped hand to clasp with Connor Mac. "Be careful in there, fellas. And know that we're so incredibly grateful for your skills and strength as a fighting force."

It sears my ego that my mate and leader is thanking another group of soldiers for heading up a mission we should be able to handle ourselves.

Should... if we had the men and the experience they do... which we don't.

I used to think the Amberloq was a fierce fighting force. When I look at Mac and the FCO enforcers readying for the incursion, I see I was wrong.

I also see the potential of what we can be.

No. What we *will* be.

Once we get through this rebellion nonsense, we will rebuild and take the Amberloq to another level.

"Okay, Mac," Honor says, stepping back from him. "Getting us in there is all you and your men. Do your thing. And be sharp, men. No one dies here today."

"At least not one of us," Hawk says. "Do what you need to in there. Lethal force is approved if necessary."

"Roger that," Mac says. "Alpha Squad, yer with me. Let's light up this rabbit hole."

~

Shadow

I miss my mates. Amberloq Hall is vacuous with no one home but me. It's also incredibly lonely. Before I lost my sight, being alone never bothered me. I loved to read or sit in silence and think or meditate. These days, being alone gives me too much uninterrupted time to think about things.

Like the loss of one of my primary senses.

Like the incessant headache that never abates.

Like the fact that at any moment I could slip into a prophetic trance and, without proper shielding and training, lose my mind and never come out of it.

"I try not to dwell, Moonshade, but it is difficult. If you knew you were doomed to suffer and die a debilitating and humiliating death you would find it difficult to be filled with sunshine too."

Moonshade wriggles against my side, her eyes closed, her paws twitching as she dreams. I rake my fingers through her long, soft fur and take comfort in her presence. She is more than my bridge to sight...

She is my companion and lifeline.

I understand she needs to sleep to grow and be healthy—I want that for her—but her slumber locks me in utter darkness. Even when she's running and rooting chaotically through her life, I don't feel as cut off from the world. When she sleeps, all that ends, and, right now, there is no one else here to replace that input of stimuli.

Amberloq Hall is both too quiet and not quiet enough without them. There is no chatter and bickering to fill the air. No sounds of cooking or sex.

This house has a voice of its own and I am not yet fluent in the language of its creaks and moans.

We lay here together, snuggling on one of the community room sofas until a noise outside startles Moonshade. She snaps awake and my world expands in an instant.

"Hello, sweeting. Did you have a nice nap?"

I sit up and adjust our position to allow her to jump down. Her intentions come to me in a rush. She wants to go outside and investigate the noise she heard.

Her claws dig into the area rug the moment her paws touch the ground. I hurry to follow, using her perception of the space to navigate around the furnishings.

"Not so fast, sweet girl. I can't keep up."

I'm not sure if it's a rush of blood from getting up too quickly, or the headache taking a violent run at me, or something else, but a tidal wave of dizziness hits, and a spearing jab of pain cleaves my skull in two.

Gasping, I drop to my knees and grab my head before it splits open. Moonshade senses my pain and turns tail to run back to me. Through her eyes, I see myself. My eyes have flipped opal white and a trail of scarlet is running down my lip.

I need help... but there is none.

The floor rises fast to meet my face as I collapse. In the fleeting moment of consciousness before I blackout, my thoughts shift to Lukas, Honor, Tundra, and Dune.

I wish they were here.

I miss my mates.

Honor

As Mac and his team set the charges on the steel door leading down into the bunker, I step over to Dune and Tundra. "Be safe, boys. I realize you're both heroes but don't take any risks you don't have to. Ruic Breard is not worth me losing one of you. You're so incredibly special to me."

Dune's mouth quirks up at the corner. "Did you ever think you'd be saying that to me?"

I hug him and tilt my face up to kiss him. "I always knew there was potential. You took the steps to make that a reality. I'm glad you did. I'm looking forward to much more of the five of us."

Dune waggles his sandy blond brows and grins. "Much more... much, much, more."

I step back and hug Tundra next. "Be careful down there, Iceman. Vikarus isn't Rhy. He's a duplicitous dick. He might be genuinely trying to help to save his skin or setting us up to fail, thinking it would be funny to send us all into a trap to get killed."

He cups my jaw and gives me a warm brush of his lips. Tundra kisses with emotion. With him, I always feel what he's saying when our mouths meet. "I'll be careful, Princess. I expect the same from you. There's no Thornebane Quint without you. We need you."

"I'm not going anywhere."

"Good, because you're special to us too."

"Hey, am I missing out on the love-in?" Lukas strides over to join us. His mental energy is aglow with anticipation. Damn, he looks fine. In black tactical gear, he's all dark and rugged and ready for battle. "Can I get in on this public display of affection?"

"Of course. There's enough to go around. I was just reminding them to be careful and to come out of this safe and well."

"Because she loves us," Dune says, grinning.

Lukas wraps his arms around me and gives me a quick kiss. "We love you too, babe. And yeah, let's all be alert in there and get home to Shadow and Moonshade. He needs us now more than ever."

There's a shared look of understanding between the four of us. No matter what happens here tonight, we need to ensure Shadow gets the help he needs. His situation as an untrained oracle is dangerous at best, lethal at worst. He needs us.

I glance over to where Calli, Jaxx, Brant, and Hawk are sharing a similar moment. When they break apart, the guys stand side by side and form a privacy screen in front of their mate. A moment later, Calli ignites and her female aflame form lights up the night.

"On my mark," Connor Mac says.

The four of us snap back to the moment at hand and get ready to breach the goblin bunker.

"Three... two... one."

Dune

Mac and the Alpha Squad blow the steel plate in the ground and then we're a go. One man grabs the bent piece of steel and reams it back while the next two guys disappear into the wall of smoke still hovering over the access opening. Tundra and I flap our wings to clear the smoke and position to join the incursion.

Vikarus told us a ladder leads fifteen feet down into a fifty-foot-long corridor. It's a dead man's chute easily defendable from inside the bunker and hard to penetrate for the intruders. Mac and three of his men are the first to head into the tunnel below.

Then it's Calli's turn.

Once her way is clear, she drops down into the opening and disappears in a glow of amber flame.

Her mates are next. Even though there are more men on Mac's team, no one tries to come between the guardians of the phoenix and her mates.

Tundra and I are next. With our natural shielding, we're the riot shields for the FCO enforcers. Tundra signals for me to go first, and I appreciate the offer.

I drop into the dark hole and flare my wings at the last moment to land silently on the concrete floor of the underground bunker.

Tundra is beside me a moment later. He drops to the position of my right flank and is as silent as the snowy owl he takes after. Lukas, Honor, and the rest of the enforcers fall in behind us.

It takes a moment for my eyes to adjust to the darkness below. And for those short moments, I am helpless to defend against anything in these hostile surroundings.

There is a scramble of activity deeper in the bunker. No doubt, the goblins have realized they're being infiltrated and are pissing their pants.

The species isn't known for their steelie countenance. A whisper over the comm brings Mac's voice into my ear. "We're in. Everyone, move out."

CHAPTER EIGHTEEN

Honor

$\mathcal{T}$he entrance of the goblin bunker drops down to a ten-foot-wide concrete tunnel. The floor and walls are smooth, and if Calli wasn't here, it would be pitch black. As we move deeper into the space I pay attention to the details given by Vikarus.

To the dragon's credit, so far at least, everything he described has been accurate.

It certainly doesn't mean I'll give him a pass.

No. He hasn't earned the benefit of the doubt. I stand by my opinion that he's a duplicitous dick. You don't get to whitewash that kind of a track record so quickly.

I don't trust the dragon and for good reason.

Our group moves as one down the sterile, gray hallway and toward the sounds of chaotic unrest. Obviously, the goblins realize their inner sanctum was violated. It'll take only another moment before they arrive.

Calli is our first line of defense.

In no way do I want to have my best friend play the part of

the Guinea pig in this organization. There's no arguing the fact she is the best equipped to withstand the hostilities we're about to face. She may not be in her full fiery phoenix form, but she's still molten hot and the heat she's radiating is incredible.

Being this close to her as we navigate the halls is like being within touching distance of the sun.

The heat is only one factor.

The illumination of her against the darkness is blinding and the air has a faint smell of char and ozone. It's like standing amid a blazing pyre in the dead of night.

It irks me a little, that I'm the Guardian of the Crown, and she's in front of this battle. I want to be a leader my mates and warriors consider an asset.

Calli is definitely an asset.

Neither jealousy nor competitiveness has any place in my world... or at least, I don't want them to.

As a barrage of gunfire is unleashed, Calli walks before us, her arms outstretched, her flaming body swallowing the metal projectiles.

She truly is magnificent.

Behind her, Hawk, Jaxx's jaguar, and Brant's massive grizzly walk tall and strong. Somehow, due to the mating bond they share, they don't feel the heat she radiates. Magic is bizarre.

Behind her are Dune and Tundra. My Biome Generals are Elbirfae and possess incredible natural shielding. That gives us an extra barrier of safety against the incoming attack.

"This way, boys. I feel portal magic calling me. It's this way." Calli points down a corridor to the right and her mates follow her without question.

When they break off, Dune and Tundra take over leading the group. They are now acting as our shield. With their wings flared wide across the ten-foot corridor, Lukas, the FCO Enforcers, and I are screened behind a wall of white and tan feathers.

"On your left," Lukas shouts.

Dune pivots toward the closed door as it swings open and goblins flood out. Lukas is right beside him, both hands raised, his guns going off in rapid-fire as goblin's drop to the bunker floor.

He is truly breathtaking in action.

I'd like to watch him longer, but Tundra is lunging in front of me, his wing jutting out as he engages with rebels coming at us from the other direction.

"I'm with you, T." I've got my blaster up and duck in tight to Tundra's wing, popping my head up to take my shots before dropping back down behind him.

From that point, all hell breaks loose.

The growl of Brant's grizzly echoes in the distance. They must be dealing with an ambush of their own. Doesn't matter. If Vikarus told us the truth, this is a one-stop-shop for destroying the Dornte rebellion all at once. We just need to dig in and take them down.

When Tundra and I take down our opponents, I tap the screen on my tactical watch and check the map. "According to Vikarus, the weapons cache is in a warehouse up here. You're with me, Tundra."

"Yes, Princess." He pivots and in two quick strides, he's not only with me but slightly ahead. I hope his position is tactical and not protective.

Yes, his shielding is a boon but I've proven I can take care of myself and be considered an equal in a fight.

"On your six, babe." Lukas's voice isn't far behind. He's there with us, and if he is, likely—I turn my head to see—yep, Dune is too.

"It's on us, boys. Let's find these weapons, destroy them, and go home."

The four of us break away and I track our position on the map to guide us deeper into the belly of the beast.

So far, it seems Vikarus hasn't screwed us over.

I'm not putting it past him and I'm not letting my guard down. The dragon screwed over his twin brother. If he can do that, there's no reason why he couldn't or wouldn't betray us for his own benefit.

Following his instructions, I lead my mates to the end of a long corridor. Before we turn into the cross-corridor, I close my eyes and reach out to sense the mental energy of anyone around.

I hold up four fingers and my mates nod their understanding. Dune and Tundra position themselves to be the first line of attack, then me, and then Lukas is there to guard the rear.

"We'll take care of the guards," Tundra says. "You two take care of the guns."

Lukas waves that off. "Let Honor take them out. We've been working on something."

"What? Here?" I ask, in a heated whisper. "Working on something isn't the same thing as perfecting something."

"True, but I'd rather you experiment on them and not us. I've seen what Creed can do with his Mind Guardian powers."

He has a point. Creed's abilities have always been more aggressive than mine. I don't like the idea of senseless death. Taking these men out by unplugging their synapses is better than flat out killing them simply for being here.

Closing my eyes, I reach out again.

I sense the four minds guarding the entrance of the weapon's keep and cut off their input. Essentially, their brains cease to send impulses to their body. One moment they're awaiting our attack and the next, they're slumping to the floor.

All four wave patterns jolt to a stop and then start up again on a lower, inactive frequency.

"I think I did it."

With a nod, Lukas holds up three fingers and then gives us the countdown.

Three... two... one.

~

Dune

The four guards go down like rocks and then Lukas counts us down. Tundra and I round the corner together. Shoulder-to-shoulder, wings flared, we provide a wall of protection for Lukas, Honor, and each other, as well.

Our shielding is in our wings, not our bodies.

A blaster shot to the chest is as painful and potentially deadly to us as it is for anyone else. Flak vests help but not as much as folding a wing in front of ourselves while we make a wall with the other.

The sting of taking fire is never welcome either. Still, it's better in the wing than not.

Except, no offensive force comes at us.

When we round the corner, Tundra and I find the four armory guards unconscious on the floor outside the weapons keep.

Did Honor do that?

By the wink and the look of pride Lukas flashes her, she did. Amazing. She's getting stronger every day. A swell of pride warms my chest. As much as I prefer to be the front line of offense to crack heads and keep Honor safe, it's good she can take care of herself too.

I want her to be able to protect herself. I want her safe. I want the chance to nurture this blooming love we share into something deep and everlasting.

After all... she loves me too.

I never thought I'd hear those words from a woman like Honor Thornebane. It's a gift—an opportunity to change my stars. I won't screw that up.

Honor loves me.

Tundra too.

Hell, even Lukas and Shadow seem to be warming up to me. One of the men on the ground rouses and sits up, pointing his weapon. I strike out with my wing and snap the man's neck. He's not a goblin but he's just as weak and uninspiring as a warrior.

"Clear," Tundra says.

I scan the corridor up and down and smile. "Clear."

Honor closes her eyes once again. How cool is it that she can sense the mental energy of people? "Clear."

Lukas takes that as his cue and presses his palm on the door of the bunker. The signature of his magic tingles over my skin as he focuses.

"The gate has been found," Mac says over the comms system. "How goes the search for the weapons?"

"Almost there," Lukas says, scowling at the door as he works. "We're accessing what we believe is the armory now. Stand by. The door was warded by the Blood Witch before her death. It'll take me a moment."

While he fights with forcing magic to do what he wants, I reach down, grab the oldest guard's hand, and drag him over to the identification scanner.

Hiking him up to his feet, I press his palm flat on the scanner. A heavy metal click signals the lock disengaging and the door slides open in front of me.

I turn to gloat. "Hey, magic man. Sometimes the simplest answer is to—"

A blast hits me in the back and sends me flying forward. I'm knocked toward the wall ten feet opposite the open door with incredible force. I barely get my hands up to save my face from impact.

It happens too quickly to understand and I'm too dazed to react beyond trying to save myself from extensive dental work.

Even still, my face hits the concrete wall with incredible force and the world goes dark.

Lukas

The door to the armory unlocks and Dune is blasted in the back by a handheld version of a launched missile. There's no time to react and no time to help him.

Thank the gods it struck him in the back.

With no impending danger, his wings were down and lying flat against his spine. That alone probably saved his life.

Honor cries out as our sandman drops to the ground unconscious.

Tundra moves to check on him, but—

"There's no time, T. We've got incoming." I throw my hands up, constructing a quick and dirty shield to seal the entranceway to the armory. "Mac, we need backup to our location."

Now that the door is open, we can see the stacks of crates and racks of weaponry we've been searching for.

"Target is acquired. I repeat, we found the cache and it's heavily guarded."

"On our way, Team Leader." Mac's voice is breathy and punctuated by the sound of thundering footsteps.

"We're coming too," Hawk says.

"Save some for us," Brants adds.

"No problem there." The opposing force is shifting for cover and seething like a ball of snakes inside the warehouse. "I've got at least two dozen hostiles and a man down."

With my palms up and casting a reinforcement on my seal holding the door, I glance over to Dune. Honor has pulled him off to the side of the door opening and has him sitting up.

189

He looks like he's still out cold.

Why the hell did he step into the doorway before we cleared the warehouse? Dumbass.

He could've gotten himself killed.

It strikes me then... how much that thought upsets me. Dune might be a pain in the ass, but he's growing on all of us. His shortcomings and overcompensation were rooted in insecurity.

We're past that now.

After all the bullshit of getting him to where we are, it would suck for him to die now.

It can't happen.

Mac comes racing around the corner with Alpha Squad and I step aside to give them a good look into the warehouse beyond the impenetrable bubble of my shield.

"Och, that's quite an arsenal they've got in there."

"Fortunately for us, they can't use it all at once. They've only got two hands."

"Except that guy." I follow Mac's pointed finger and cringe at the f-ugly six-winged, four-armed rebel coming out from behind a warehouse lift truck.

"What the fuck is that?"

"Highly disturbing," Brant says joining us. "How do we get in there to end this thing?"

"I guess that's my cue." I raise my hands and check with the FCO team and the quint as they gather in front of the seal of the door. "Are you guys ready for this?"

"I was born ready," Brant says. "Drop the shield and let the games begin."

Once the incursion teams take cover to the sides of the open door, I do as Brant suggests. Dropping the seal is easy, pushing inside when more than a dozen armed combatants are trying to keep you out isn't as easy.

"Follow me, gentlemen," Calli says, taking point and upsizing to her full phoenix form the moment she steps into the warehouse.

The heat she radiates pushes back the rebel forces and the fiery flame that envelops her outstretched wings offers enough cover to allow our squadrons the chance to slip inside and take ground.

Jaxx's jaguar jolts off to the right, Brant's bear takes the left, and Hawk stays tight to their mate.

Tundra and two of the FCO enforcers take a run at the doorway and launch into the air. They pump their wings and arch up and over the flaming crown of Calli's phoenix.

Gunfire sounds off in a steady stream, but Tundra rules in the air. I know that firsthand. It wasn't so long ago that I had my guns pointed directly at him and was firing as he was flying to attack me.

Funny how the universe changes our perspective on things. With that in mind, I turn to check in on Honor and Dune. Our boy has his eyes open now but still looks like he's seeing stars.

"Hey, welcome back," I say rushing to crouch next to him to take a quick check of his vitals. "You took quite a hit there."

"Was it a bomb? It felt like a bomb."

I release his wrist and lean in to take a look at his pupils. "It wasn't a bomb, but it was an explosive. What the hell were you doing standing in front of an open door before we had a chance to clear it for danger?"

"I don't remember. What's my name? Are you my daddy?"

I blink, and for a brief moment I'm worried that he might be serious, but then his expression cracks into a wide grin, and his body starts to jiggle with amusement.

"You're an asshole. and here I thought you might actually be hurt."

"Oh, I'm hurting, but that isn't a limiting factor on whether or not I'm an asshole."

Honor rolls her eyes and straightens to stand. Each of us

grips under one of Dune's arms and we lift him to his feet. "What did I say about not getting yourself killed? It was only fifteen minutes ago, and yet here we are scraping you off the concrete."

"In my defense, you said not to be a hero. I've never been a hero."

I throw his arm over my shoulder and make sure he's steady. "By the looks of things in there, everything is under control. Let's get you shuffling towards the exit. Can you walk?"

He glances down at his boots as if he's unsure and needs to check on the answer to that himself. When he's able to propel himself in a forward motion, he smiles up at me and waggles his brow. "Oh yeah, I've still got it."

Honor chuckles. "You're crazy."

Despite what Dune says, his motor coordination isn't one hundred percent. Sure he's making a joke of it now, but I'd feel a lot better if he wasn't leaning so heavily on me to stay upright.

"This is Team Leader. If you don't need us, Honor and I have Dune and will head up to the surface."

"Roger that, Team Leader," Mac says.

"Always the first to leave the party," Hawk adds.

I chuckle, adjust my hold on Dune, and draw my weapon in case we run into any hostiles during our exit. "Don't hate, Barron. Some of us just know when it's time to leave."

A thundering boom sounds off behind us and we stagger to the side to stay standing.

"Hawk? What the fuck was that?"

It takes a moment before the response comes back to us and then there's a rush of chatter and excitement over the comms. "Calli overheated the gunpowder. This place is going to blow. Everyone fall back and get out now."

CHAPTER NINETEEN

Dune

The three of us are almost back to the original dark tunnel by the time the rest of our teams catch up. Behind us, it's like the world is exploding in a rapid succession of violent detonations.

"Wow, when Calli does something, she takes it all the way," Honor says, pushing Lukas and me toward the ladder to get out of here.

"She's always been a bit heavy-handed with justice," Jaxx says, carrying an unconscious FCO Enforcer in a fireman's hold over his shoulder.

"Let me take him," Tundra says as he arrives at the base of our escape route. "I'll fly him up instead of having you try to climb the ladder with him."

"Have we got everyone?" Mac shouts, rushing to join our group. His deep russet hair is singed in a few places and by the charcoal on his face and the way he's shouting, I'm guessing he was close to an explosion. "I can't hear a feckin' thing. Niah, make sure we've got everyone."

"Roger, Alpha-1," Niah says, coming up fast from behind. "Let's hear it, men. Sound off your squadrons."

"Team Leader and Alpha-1 are secure," Lukas says, helping Mac to the ladder.

"Alpha-2 ready to exit," a brute of a soldier says behind me.

The roll call continues through Alpha Squad, then Beta, and then Delta. By the time we're all topside, it seems everyone is accounted for.

"Great work, everyone," Hawk says, pulling the last of his FCO employees from the opening of the bunker. "Mission accomplished. I think we can honestly say both the rift and the weapon's cache are secure."

"The rift is toast," Brant says. "We made damned sure of that."

"How did they even access enough power to open a rift without the Phoenix Quint?" Honor asks. "Calli's told me the story about the soul crystals and how difficult it was to open the rift in Pennsylvania. How did Hawk's brother manage it here?"

"Hunter hasn't been very forthcoming with the answers to that yet," Hawk says. "But I promise you, we'll find out. Maybe now that we found and destroyed the access he helped build, he'll be a little more cooperative with the details."

"He couldn't get any *less* cooperative," Lukas says.

Hawk nods. "That's true."

"And we're sure the weapons cache has been dealt with?" I ask. "It will look bad to say we've got a handle on the military strength of the rebellion only to find out that their firepower is greater than we thought."

Calli chuckles and waves her fingers at me. "Nothing to worry about there. I melted everything down and even while things were exploding and the evacuation had begun, I took another look around to make sure the job was done right."

"Was that the job of eliminating the weapons or blowing us

up?" one of the FCO guys asks, flopping back on the grass laughing.

Calli shrugs on one of her fireproof dresses and frees her ponytail from the collar. "What can I say, I'm a multi-tasker."

Jaxx pulls her shoes out of their backpack and hands them to her. "Yes, you are, Kitten. Now, how about we go home, have a shower, and check on our wolf and our baby boy?"

Calli grins. "Sounds perfect."

I take a cue from the military men lying on the grass recovering and make an effort to collect myself.

Damn. Things got dicey down there.

I legitimately could have died.

Shoving the reality of that way down deep, I focus on what's important: building a life with my mates, building an Amberloq force that can secure the crown, and becoming the man I know I can be for as long as I have life beating in my chest.

Tundra

"Home sweet home." The four of us are covered in dirt, smell like a bonfire, and are more than a little worn out. I drop our duffel bag inside the door as we arrive home at Amberloq Hall. "I vote for a shower, a hot meal, and early to bed."

"To bed or to sleep?" Dune asks.

I glance back at him. "Seriously? You can barely walk. An evening of rest would do you some good."

He scoffs at me as if I spat in his food. "In my experience, rest is highly overrated. Live each day like there is no tomorrow. That's my motto."

Honor chuckles and heads into the community room. "Then you're either going to have to live this day with one of the others or get close and personal with your palm. I'm tagging out —Oh, dear."

It's the shock in her voice that tells me something's wrong and I jog to catch up with her.

"What's wrong?" I ask, coming through the entranceway. There's a stranger in our home. An elderly man with short blond hair and a trimmed beard is sitting on the sofa. "May I ask who you are and what you're doing here?"

Lukas rushes in to join us, his boots half unlaced and hanging loose. "Demarco? What are you... thank you for coming."

The man dips his chin and rises to greet Lukas. The two shake hands and then Lukas seems to realize the rest of us are still wondering who this is. "May I tell them?"

The man nods. "Yes, of course."

Lukas steps back and holds his hand out for Honor to come stand beside him. "Demarco is the contact I mentioned in the other realm who I thought might know how to help Shadow."

This is the first I've heard of it, but Honor seems to know what he's talking about. She reaches forward to offer him her hand. "Thank you so much for coming."

"I wish I could say it was a pleasure, but under the circumstances, I'm afraid that would be in bad taste."

"Where's Shadow?" Lukas asks. "Did you have a chance to meet him?"

"If he is the elf with purple hair who I found unconscious on the floor, then yes, I've seen him, though we haven't exactly met."

"Unconscious? Where is he now?"

"I gave him a powerful sedative and closed him and his little wolf in the closest bedroom I found. You have many beds in this home with no people living here."

Honor waves that away. "Is Shadow all right?"

"No. Not in the slightest. Luckily, I came when I did. The

progression of his mental fatigue has started taking its toll. We need to start on a self-care regimen immediately or his cognitive reason will be lost."

Lukas looks torn between relief and panic. "But you think you can help him?"

"To a point. I can certainly help slow the decay of his mental stability, but the life of an untrained oracle is tenuous at best. Are you certain you wish to involve yourself in all that entails? If you wish, I can remove him and do what I can back on my mountain."

Lukas shakes his head. "He stays here with us. He is ours to care for and I won't ship him away when he needs us most. Can you stay and help us until we have a plan on what we need to do?"

Demarco points to the small carpetbag on the floor by the door. "After all you've done for me, I am ever at your disposal."

Lukas steps forward and pulls the man against his chest. "Thank you, my friend. You can't know how much this means to me."

The man offers him a private smile. "You of all people must know that's not true. I know exactly what it means to you. I've been there too."

~

Honor

After settling Demarco into a bedroom on the main floor, I leave Lukas to talk through the details about Shadow and Tundra to start cooking us something hot for a late meal. With that under control, I take Dune to soak in the milk baths in the Amberloq Training Center across the back courtyard.

"The medicinal benefits of the milk baths are long-praised as one of the reasons Amberloq warriors seem indestructible.

Their regenerative power might even rival Calli's phoenix tears."

"That's a big claim," Dune says, shuffling in as I hold the door for him.

"It is, but if it holds true, with any luck, you'll be fighting fit by morning."

The bathing area is a long, rectangular room with eight sunken troughs in the floor. The milky water that fills them is heated by a natural spring that runs beneath the grounds.

There is a decorative skylight overhead but because it's well past the rise of the second moon, the only thing we see is the silver glow of the night sky.

"Here. Let me help you with that vest." Careful not to touch his back, I unstrap the wide Velcro bands wrapping around Dune's ribs. Slowly, I ease the Kevlar pinny over his head and set it on one of the benches against the long wall. "You took quite a hit tonight."

"The hit came out of nowhere. I didn't have time to react or protect myself."

"Thankfully, your wings shielded you from the worst of it."

"Yeah, lucky me."

His wings are different than mine. His are heavy, not retractable, and branch out of his muscled shoulder blades. They emerge high on his back and almost act as another set of appendages.

Mine are sheer, eject from the ridge on both sides of my spine, and retract when not in use. They flutter and allow me to fly, but I can't bring them around my body and use them as shields or to strike people as he can.

People tell me how beautiful my ebony and teal wings are—and they are—but so are his. Dune's wings are powerful, graceful, and his feathers are as soft as the most precious down.

"Open your wings so I can have a look."

He turns so I can see his back and slowly flexes his wings

open. His back is black and purple and looks like he was hit by a missile—which he was.

My stomach churns.

The reality of that grips my heart.

This life we live is dangerous and I could lose any one of the four of them at any time. They are my warriors—mine to love as well as protect—and I'm not strong enough to keep them safe.

Yet.

"That bad, is it?"

Dune's joking tone doesn't lighten my mood. I step around his majestic wings and study his chest for any other injuries. "I'm so sorry you were hurt tonight."

With a gentle finger, he lifts my chin and meets my gaze. "Why are you crying?"

I bring my fingers up to my cheeks and capture the warm tears. I didn't realize I was crying, but it makes sense. "I hate to see you so broken and bruised. It hurts my heart."

He unstraps my vest, pulls it over my head, and tosses it over onto his. My wings are retracted, so when he slides his hands under the hem of my shirt and around to caress my back, his callused hands meet nothing but smooth skin.

Oh, and my spinal ridges.

I gasp as he trails a heated touch up those ridges. Every cell in my body wakes up and I arch forward, pressing myself against his solid frame. "I know I said I was out for the night, but how about we get naked and soak for a while together. If more comes of it, that's great. If not, I could still use some time to relax and heal with you."

"I think that's an inspired idea." He pulls my shirt up and over my head, and I reach down and unfasten his pants. My bra is the next to go, and then he kicks off his boots. He winces as he bends for his socks, so I kneel before him and help him out.

By the time we're both naked, I've forgotten my exhaustion

from earlier and am hoping more does come of it... though I won't push because he needs to heal.

He's lowered himself onto the edge of one of the troughs and is easing into the milky bath when I finish setting my clothes aside. He winces as he flares his wings forward so he can submerge in the healing waters.

With his shoulders and back in the water and his chest mostly submerged, he settles. His turquoise eyes roll back in his head, and he lets out an exhale of pure bliss.

I watch him for a moment and the surface of my skin rises in goosebumps. "Dune?"

"Yes, Princess?"

"I know these are built for one person but if you think there might be room, I'd like to join you."

He opens his eyes and raises a hand to help me into the waters of his tub. "I was just thinking I may never get out. Now I'm quite sure I won't."

Dune is a big tease, but as the words escape his lips there's not a doubt in my mind that he means them. That's good. I'm glad he's finding the bath so soothing.

With as much care as I can offer, I ease into the tub facing him. There is space between his thigh and the wall of the trough for me to step down to join him.

I consider setting myself up at the opposite end of the trough and facing him as I have with Lukas but decided instead to stretch out on my stomach so that I'm lying on his chest. "Is this all right?"

"It's perfection."

We lay like that, simply enjoying the contact of chest against chest, hips against hips, and with our legs woven together beneath the surface of the warm, healing milk. With his arms gently folded over my back, I feel cherished and safe.

I close my eyes and soak in the moment.

The Dune of old would've already made an off-color joke or

pass at me. Honestly, he could make a pass at me right now and I'd agree to pretty much anything.

"This is nice," he says, his voice low and husky.

I adjust my cheek against his collarbone but can't bring myself to open my eyes. I'm so relaxed. Lying here with him is the most relaxed I've felt in weeks.

I must have dozed off because I wake to the sensation of his hands gently caressing up and down the line of my spine.

"Sorry. Did I fall asleep on you?"

"You did but there's nothing to be sorry about. This has been, without a doubt, the most incredible moment I've ever shared with a woman."

"With me asleep and us not even having sex?"

He chuckles beneath me, the vibration of his amusement jiggling us both. "I must be losing my edge."

I trail a gentle finger down the muscled plain of his pectoral and play with his nipple. "No complaints here. Well, maybe one."

"Oh, and what would that be?"

"First, how are you feeling? Do you think the milk bath is working?"

He shifts a little beneath me twisting his shoulders to stretch his back and hips. "Definitely working. The aching agony has dulled down to a bit tender. I feel quite a bit better."

"I'm glad to hear that. If you're feeling up to it, I'd like to maybe make you feel even better." Lifting my head, I meet his gaze and bite my bottom lip. "You won't have to do any work. Just lie back and focus on feeling better."

The coy smile that softens his face sends a warm rush to my core. "Are you suggesting some sexual healing?"

"Would you be open to it if I am?"

"I'm quite sure you can already feel the answer to that question probing at your belly."

"All good ideas come from somewhere." I grin and shift my

weight from lying prone on top of him to climbing his abdomen and straddling his hips.

He slides his hands up my back as his gaze rises to meet mine. The lust and admiration in his eyes mean so much to me. Men have often found me attractive—as a mind guardian it's easy to know that for certain—but to Dune, the beauty is more than what he sees, it's what I mean to him and the future he's starting to believe in.

As we kiss, I shift until his erection presses at my entrance and grip his muscled shoulders. Using my hold for leverage, I take him inside me.

The penetration is welcome, the intrusion delicious.

He groans, flexing his hips as his tongue strokes against mine.

I ride him in languid, greedy strokes, meeting his kiss with passion as the urgency inside me builds.

He gasps as he breaks our kiss, tugging at my bottom lip, pulling the sensitive flesh between his teeth. His hunger is erotic and tender and reverent.

I love the feeling of his body inside mine and that intimacy increases as we move together. My insides tighten around him, the clenching of my need burning slow and deep.

His hands shift down to my hips and he grips my sides. He takes control of our strokes first lifting me until he's almost out and then lowering me, sinking deeper.

We continue like that, slow at first but building in rhythm and urgency. I love the ache that I feel when he's moving inside me like this. It makes me crave more of him... more *from* him.

Milky spring water splashes between us, the sound punctuated by our gasping breaths.

"Oh, yes," I groan as my body begins to tighten. I arch back as my orgasm takes hold, and my greedy muscles squeeze his cock.

My climax ripples through me in waves.

He drives into me again and again gripping my hips with bruising force, but I don't care. With a shouting exhale, he stiffens beneath me, his head tossing back as his body constricts in gasps of pleasure.

With the aftershocks of my orgasm still pulsing inside me, I collapse against his chest and ride the rise and fall of his ragged breathing.

"Princess..." he gasps. "That was incredible."

It was. I know Dune has always considered sex to be the physical exertion of bodies coming together solely for the sake of pleasure, but that was next-level intimacy and connection for both of us.

"Thank you. That was perfect."

His arms come over me once again, followed by the extra protection of his wings folding to cocoon us together. "I love you, Princess. I don't say that lightly and you don't have to say it back if you're not there yet, but I could have died tonight, and you never would've known. I love you, Honor, and I'm proud to be in your life."

I tilt my head back and read the sincerity in those turquoise eyes of his. "I'm incredibly relieved you didn't die tonight, sweety, because I love you too—soul deep."

The smile that earns me will keep me warm for days and weeks to come. Resting my cheek on his chest, I close my eyes. "And yes, this is really nice."

CHAPTER TWENTY

Lukas

"Hey, when did you get back?"
I bend down and kiss Moonshade's nose before switching my gaze to Shadow. He's been asleep for the hour since we got home and despite Demarco's reassurances, I admit I was getting worried.

"Hey yourself. So, what's this I hear about you collapsing again while we were gone?"

"Did I?"

"Don't you remember?"

He rolls onto his back, stretches an arm above his head, and seems to be reflecting. When he looks up at me like this, it's hard to believe he is suffering from such a serious, life-threatening ailment.

"The last thing I remember is being downstairs with a headache and getting up to let Moonshade out for a run. I got dizzy when I got up too fast from the sofa. I'm guessing it wasn't just a head rush?"

"It might've been, but likely not. The good news is, a friend of mine from the Human Realm who knows about the late development of oracle powers arrived in time to find you and get you sorted out."

"A friend of yours? You never mentioned anything."

"I didn't want to say anything until I knew for sure he'd be willing to help but he is and he's here, so that's a good thing."

Shadow holds up his hand and I take it squeezing our palms together. "That's a very good thing and great news to wake up to. Thank you."

"Of course. I told you before, you're not alone. We're going to figure this out together and the five of us are going to have a long, happy life together. All you need to do is trust me and not give up hope."

"I trust you. If there's anyone in the two realms who can make things happen, it's you."

I chuckle at the absolute conviction in his voice. "And if not me directly, having two kings, a princess, Hawk Barron, and the Phoenix of the Fae Realms in the family helps get things done."

"There's that too." He reclaims his hand and sits up. "Speaking of which, how did things go tonight? Did you get things done?"

"We did. It got a little dicey when Dune got shot by a hand-launched missile and Calli overheated the gunpowder in the armory, but other than that it was smooth sailing."

"Is Dune all right?"

"Never been better," Dune says, coming in to join us. "I was a bit battered and bruised but nothing an hour in the healing waters of the milk baths couldn't take care of. I'm as good as new—better than new."

I recognize the glow of happiness in his eyes and smile at Honor standing just inside the door. "I take it the quiet time recuperating in the baths went well?"

"Very well," she says. "We need to do that more often. I can't

JL MADORE

even tell you how rejuvenating it was to spend quiet time lounging in the healing waters."

"Just quiet time?" I asked teasing.

"We may have gotten a little vocal near the end," she says, smiling.

Dune chuckles. "Maybe just a little."

Tundra leans in the open doorway, takes in Shadow sitting up in bed, and then Dune standing tall and fit in the center of the room. "It looks like things are improving around here."

"Thankfully so," I say, breathing a sigh of relief. "What's the word on getting a bite to eat? How is our late-night stew going?"

"All I need are the people who want to eat."

"I could eat," Shadow says.

"I've worked up quite an appetite," Dune says.

Honor giggles. "I'm starving."

"Then it's settled," I say, standing and tugging Shadow to his feet. "It's Musketeer time."

Dune and Tundra look confused by that, and I realize they probably don't have a frame of reference. "The Three Musketeers was a book written in the Human Realm that was later adapted into movies and a television show. We'll watch it so you can see for yourself, but the gist of what I was saying is their motto. All for one and one for all."

"That's a great motto for us," Tundra says, coming over to help Shadow get his bearings. "I have a feeling it's going to take all of us to overcome what we've got hanging over our heads."

Dune wraps an arm around Honor's back and brings her in so the five of us are standing in an intimate circle. "I have a feeling you're right, Iceman. We've still got to track down Ruic Breard, wipe out the rebellion, build up the Amberloq and figure out Shadow's oracle powers and what his prophecy means."

Honor shrugs. "Yeah, there's lots on our to-do list but we've learned a lot over the past weeks. We're a great team. We've got strength, power, heart, wisdom, and dedication to the future. Whatever needs doing, we'll get there."

"We will." Shadow slides one arm around my back and the other around Tundra's.

"There's still much to do, no question, but we've got this." Tundra wraps his free hand around Dune's hip and then Dune pulls Honor to his other side.

When Honor and I link up, the five of us are in a huddle and everything in the realm seems to settle into place. "The Thornebane Quint is going to rock this realm," she says, "and anyone who thinks differently is in for a rude awakening."

I nod. "You bet your beautiful ass they are."

<u>Author Notes</u>

Written on 11/22/2021

I hope you're enjoying the continuation of the Guardians of the Fae Realms through the love story of Honor, Lukas, Shadow, Tundra, and Dune. What was meant to be a trilogy turned into a four-book addition to the series.

There was more story to tell and more moments that the characters wanted to share. Sometimes that happens and I just let things unfold as they are meant to. So, a quick FB message to my cover designer—the fabulous Sanja Gombar—and voila we are now headed into Honor Empowered.

Don't miss what happens next with Honor and her mates as she takes the rebels of the realm by the balls and sets things in motion for Dornte's recovery from the Wars of Power.

Grab the fourth and final book in Honor's harem here.

FYI: I always intended to write the birth of the baby phoenix from the perspectives of Calli, Jaxx, Kotah, Hawk, and Brant. If you want to read that story, I'm going to offer it as bonus content to the fans who follow my newsletter. If you're not on my newsletter list, come join the fun by clicking **HERE.**

Hugs to all,
JL

<u>Find Me</u>
My Direct Sales Site: Shopify
My books
Web page – www.jlmadore.com
Email – jlmadorewrites@gmail.com
Newsletter – JL Series Updates

Four amazing men. One fae princess to bind them. And a destiny to realize.

I had a rocky start to my appointment as Guardian of the Crown, but I'm resilient and determined to seize the reigns of my destiny—even if it means going up against an evil man like Ruic Breard. But when a shocking discovery threatens my position—and the bonds I've created—I worry I won't be enough to lead my mates to the victory the quadrant needs.

Lukas, Tundra, Dune, and Shadow believe in me and are committed to help me stabilize the Dornte Quadrant.

But what if their confidence isn't enough? What if *I'm* not enough?

Claim your copy now: Honor Empowered

ALSO BY JL MADORE

Book 1 – Captured by the Magi

Book 2 – Jesse and the Magi Vault

Book 3 – The Makings of a Magi Knight

Book 4 – Clash with the Magi Council

Book 5 – The Unstoppable Storme

Club Sanguine

Book 1 – Moonstone Maelstrom

Book 2 - Sunstone Sacrifice

JL's More Traditional M/F, M/M, or Menage

The Watchers of the Gray Series (Paranormal)

Book 1 – Watcher Untethered – Zander

Book 2 – Watcher Redeemed – Kyrian

Book 3 – Watcher Reborn – Danel

Book 4 – Watcher Divided – Phoenix

Book 5 – Watcher United – Seth

Book 6 – Watcher Compelled – Bo

Book 7 – Watcher Unfeigned – Brennus

Book 8 – Watcher Exposed – Taharqa

The Scourge Survivor Series (Fantasy)

Book 1 – Blaze Ignites

Book 2 – Ursa Unearthed

Book 3 – Torrent of Tears

Book 4 – Blind Spirit

Book 5 – Fate's Journey

Book 6 – Savage Love – epilogue novella

Aliens of Atlantis Series (Sci-Fi)

Book 1 – Taryn's Tiderider

Book 2 – Kai's Captive

Book 3 – Alyandra's Shadow

www.ingramcontent.com/pod-product-compliance
Lightning Source LLC
Chambersburg PA
CBHW020320260626
47156CB00004B/1302